The Probability of Violet and Luke

JESSICA SORENSEN

D1512296

Prologue

Luke

Who knew a fucking phone call could be so complicated. It should have been a piece of cake for me. All these years spent hating my mother—this is what I've been waiting for. Finally, I'd get some form of revenge for all the years of torment, drug injections, the fucking mind games she loved to play with me, and all the other shittiness that made up my childhood. To this day, I still haven't even started to fully accept or admit all the stuff she did to me. This should be the moment when I let it all go. Move on. Start over. Except I feel guilty, like I'm a child doing something wrong.

I feel sick to my stomach.

All twisted inside.

And I know it's because of *her*. Everything she engrained into my head is surfacing. All the stuff she said to me when I was a child that kept my lips shut. The shame. The embarrassment, not just because she's my mother, but for myself because of what she turned me into.

"You always need to listen to me Lukey," my mother used to say. "I know what's best for you, more than anyone else does. You always need to do what I say, otherwise you won't survive this life. And you can't tell anyone what we do in our house. It's no one else's business." She'd pause and pet my head like I was her dog. "Besides, if they found out the things you've done, you'd be in a lot of trouble too."

I was about eight-years-old the first time she said this to me and even then it didn't feel right. The things she made me do... the way she would hold me for hours, murmuring high, incoherent songs, smoothing her hand over my head, kissing my cheek, begging me to shoot her up again. Wrong. It all felt wrong and disgusting. But the more she said it was my fault, the more it seemed like maybe it was true. How could it not be? She was my mother after all and mothers aren't supposed to lie to their children.

So I listened to her. Day in and day out, I kept my lips shut. Sometimes I would try to run away from the house, because I couldn't take it anymore. But she'd always find me and I started wondering if it was her I needed to survive against. Eventually, I found a way to cope. Drinking and sex, they helped me forget and let me get the control I craved over my life.

Shaking past thoughts from my head, I sigh with the phone clutched in my hand. Yeah, I know that my mother's insane, that she ruined my childhood, fucked up my head. So turning her into the police should be easier than this and I'm angry with myself that it's not.

Still, in the end, I picture Violet, beautiful green eyes, full lips, long waves of red and black hair, a sexy tattooed body, a diamond stud in her nose, and the sadness and pain in her expression the last time I held her in my arms. That's what helps me dial the police station.

"Hello, Albany County Police Department," the secretary answers. When I hesitate she adds, "Is anyone there?"

I clear my throat again and again, but I force myself to be strong and fight through my nerves, each one connected to something that happened to me when I was younger. "Yeah, I'd like to report some information about the Hayes' murder." As soon as the words leave my lips, I feel twenty times better, the guilt becoming lighter. I just wish doing this could erase the past, but nothing will do that. Nothing will ever get me Violet back. What's done is done and I can't ever change it.

Violet

Life. I hate it. More than ever. And destiny, it can go to hell. I fucking hate destiny.

As his callous hands are on me, feeling my skin, making me internally cringe, I wish I'd never met the bastard known as destiny. Then maybe I'd never gotten a taste of the other side of life, the good side. Then maybe *this* wouldn't be so hard.

As much as I'm panicking on the inside, on the outside I am the calm, collected Violet. The one that can fake smile at the drop of a hat. The one that can charm anyone. Even when the pain comes, when my legs bump into side of the bed as I'm forced down onto my knees, I don't so much as flinch. I'm dead on the outside, stone cold, while on the inside my heart is racing so fast, I feel light-headed and woozy. Everything's moving so quickly, so blurry, I can't sort through my emotions, which is a good thing. It makes it impossible to tell what I'm feeling and makes this moment bearable, less painful, less shameful.

Still, as hands continue to wander over me, whispers of *owing for messing up, this is the cost, I'm all you got* fills my ears and kills my soul, bit by bit, piece by piece. As my head is forced downward, I find myself wishing there was a pause button where I could freeze time, step out of this place and erase what's about to happen to me.

Yes, there are a shitload of moments in my life that I wish I could do over. That time I didn't study for my Calculus test, because Preston needed me to deal for him for the first time. The time I went downstairs in the middle of the night and my parents were murdered, while I survived. The night I ran from Luke. This one.

Each has had consequences; some more severe than others. And unfortunately I painfully understand that do-overs don't exist, at least one's where you can erase the past and start over. And for the most part, excluding my parents' deaths, I've never put too much thought into do-overs, placing most of the blame for the shit fest known as my life onto destiny.

But it's been two months since I left Luke and the apartment that felt more like a home to me than any other place I ever lived. And even though it still makes me sick thinking about how our pasts are tangled together, starting long before we even met, part of me wishes I'd done things differently. Two months of pure hell with moments packed with whispered threats and callous hands where I've lost track of Violet Hayes, the version Luke Price brought out. She died the second she chose to come back to Preston's house, because she was hurting and couldn't think of anywhere else to go. And I'm not sure if she'll ever live again.

This time I can't blame what's happening to me on destiny. Only my pride, my wounded heart, and the choice I made that led me to countless bad choices, all of which can never be erased.

None of this can.

Chapter 1

Violet

I'm on the brink of losing consciousness, fading in and out as two months of bad decisions weigh me down and push me further into the water. My entire body is drenched, my lungs about to combust, yet I don't come up for air. I freely accept the lack of life inside me and allow myself to stay there, until I feel light and weightless. A second or two longer. That's all I need. I can do it. Feel the comfort for just one more moment before I have to return to the painful reality of my life and what I am.

Just one more second.

Hold your breath.

Keep it in.

Trap the pain.

Drown it out.

Don't think.

Breathe.

Don't live.

Sometimes I wonder what would happen if I took it one step too far. Stayed under the water one breath too long. Inched a step too close to the edge. Drove just a little too fast down the road. Death. Would it hurt? Or would it be weightless? Liberating? At the very end, would it be better than life? Would I finally, at the very end, be able to breathe freely again? The only way I'll ever know is to go through with it—fall off that edge. Go too fast. Sink to the bottom and never come up for air. I'm so close to finding out, yet I'm not ready to fully seal my fate just yet.

So gripping onto the edge of the bathtub, I drag myself up out of the water, gasping for air, my lungs gratefully aching. I sit up, half in, half out of the water, inhaling, exhaling, blood pumping through my veins and mixing with the adrenaline. My emotions are still numb and I focus on getting that next breath of air. But the longer I breathe, the easier it becomes, and the more my mind starts to awaken. Feelings and thoughts of my parents' deaths arise, stabbing at my heart. Their murders. And the thing that nearly kills me every time I think about it. Every minute. Every second. Every damn day—it consumes me.

Luke Price. The one guy—the only person—I've ever let in. The only person I've ever felt safe with. And now that's all gone. He's gone. Taken away—stolen—by destiny's sick and warped humor. Letting us meet for the first time, then allowing us to discover that we've been connected with each other long before we first met. Revealing that his mother was one of the people responsible for my parents' murders. That all along, we could never have ended up together. Even though destiny let us think that it was meant to be from the moment I fell out that window and kicked him in the face. And now, I'm left feeling worse than I ever have in my entire life.

And now I'm left feeling worse than I've ever have in my entire life. Before Luke, I didn't know what it was like to have someone care about me and to understand how it felt to care about someone else and I'm learning really quickly that it's difficult turning my emotions off when I know how amazing things can feel.

But I keep trying to push through, if for nothing else, then to see this through the end. See someone finally pay for my parents' deaths. It might be impossible, though, since there's still another person involved—another person that is still unknown. I hate not knowing, yet at the same time, I loathe knowing who one of them is, especially since there hasn't been any justice yet. Hate that it ruined my shot at happiness and I despise myself for thinking about it that way. It feels selfish. My parents are dead and I should only be thinking about justice for them, yet I can't stop thinking about how Luke made me feel—content and happy. Something I hadn't had since I was five-years-old. I want it back, almost as much as I want justice for my parents. And that feels wrong; makes me feel like my parents would hate me if they were still around. And maybe they do now. Maybe they hate me from the graves I've never yet even paid a visit to, simply because I can't bring myself to go there.

"Violet, what the hell are you doing in there!" Preston, the foster father I had from the ages of fifteen until I became eighteen and an adult, bangs on the door. He's eight years older than me, but doesn't mind the age difference, and uses it to his advantage all the time. He didn't use to be so interested in me, well not to this extreme. But then his wife left him and now all he seems to see is me. It makes me sick to my stomach, just hearing the sound of his voice because it reminds me of everything that's happened the last two months I've been living here. Rent doesn't come free and Preston won't accept money. So I deal to pay rent and then my body pays him for any mistakes I make along the way.

I hate myself for letting despair kill me enough that I allow stuff to happen.

"I'm taking a bath," I reply, brushing my hands over my wet hair and letting my head fall back against the rim of the tub as vomit burns at the back of my throat.

"Well, it you don't get out soon, I'm going to have to pick the lock and come in and make you get out," he says through the door with amusement in his tone. And desire. Lust. Need. .

I hate him.

I need him.

I wish I was somewhere else.

"I'll be out in just a few," I holler back, watching the faucet drip and ripple the water. I put my foot up on the brim of the tub and stare at the yellowish bruises covering my shin all the way up to me thigh. But as the images rise of where they came from, I shake my head and put my wall back up. I refuse to think about them. I need to survive no matter what happens, like how I did for most of my life, in and out of foster homes. After all, I've had worse.

"You should get dressed out here," he tells me, the sound of his voice making the bruises on my flesh sting. "It could be another payback for that eighth you lost last week."

I cringe at his reminder. Last week I messed up badly. I was distracted, knowing that the semester would be starting in a few days and that Luke and I would have to see each other again in the hallways and probably in class. I ended up giving some guy an eighth without collecting the cash first and he took off without paying, totally screwing me over.

"I thought I was going to sell for you on Saturday and Sunday for that." I don't bother mentioning that I already did something else to make up for it, only because I'm afraid I'll throw up if I say it aloud. I slump back and stare at the ceiling, willing myself not to be affected by his words, not be affected by the vile sensation manifesting in the pit of my stomach.

"You're becoming a real downer, Violet Hayes," he says. "Life would be so much easier if you'd just relax and do what I tell you."

"I do that already," I reply through gritted teeth. I've never been a fan of hearing my last name, or even telling people it. It reminds me too much of my mother and father and how they died. The only person that's said it where it didn't bother me was Luke. Usually I'd chew Preston out for using it, but lately I've been too emotionally drained to put up a good fight.

I only breathe freely when I hear Preston walk away from the door. Then I get out of the bathtub and dry off my pruney skin with a towel before putting on a purple tank top, a black vest, and matching pants. I tousle my hair with some gel, put lip-gloss and some kohl liner on, then head out of the bathroom, feeling a little high from the adrenaline rush I got from almost drowning myself in the bathtub.

I grab a Pop Tart from the cupboard and a bottle of water from the fridge, hoping that Preston will be cooperative when I ask him for a ride to school. *Please be cooperative.*

But he's not in his room, which probably means he's down under the house in the crawl space, where he keeps his drugs. The entrance is always locked but I wouldn't go down there anyway. The last thing I want to do is go down into some creepy, small, narrow space below the house, alone with him. So I go into the living room and put my boots on, taking my time as I wait for him to come out.

The trailer that we live in is fairly clean, although it does smell like cigarette smoke and weed. Still, there's no garbage lying around and everything is organized and in place. I've lived in foster homes where cleanliness was nonexistent and filth, garbage and dust coated everything. It wasn't ideal.

"So what are you up to today?" Preston asks as he strolls into the house, slipping on a plaid hooded jacket and then dusting some dirt out of his hair.

My fingers twitch with this aching urge to ball my hand into a fist and punch the casualness off his face. But I bury the urge and zip up my knee-high boot, then get to my feet, reaching for my bag. "I actually need a ride to class,

unless you just want to lend me your car for the day."
Please say a simple yes with no strings attached.

"You know I hate doing that unless it's for dealing," he says, leaning against the doorframe and crossing his arms, giving me that look—the one that comes before he asks me to do something for him. "Then I'm just stuck here without a vehicle."

I swing the handle of my bag over my shoulder. "Well, can you give me a ride then? That way you'll still have your car." School has only been going for a few days and it's already becoming a pain in the ass to get there. I should have just gotten a dorm room again, but I stupidly waited to long, thinking I was going to just live in the apartment with Luke, Seth, and Greyson, but that brilliant plan went to shit.

Preston ruffles his hair into place as he crosses the room and comes to a stop in front of me, too close and I can smell him—I hate the smell of him. "I hate doing that because then I have to wait around for a couple of hours to pick you up."

"Don't you have anything in town you need to do?" I subtly lean away from him, his scent becoming too nauseating.

He shakes his head. "Not really." He reaches for his car keys on the coffee table. "But I do have shit to do over at Dan's."

My mood plummets. "Dan the pervert?"

He nonchalantly shrugs, swinging the keychain around his finger. "You say pervert. I say a guy who just likes to have fun." He winks. "Just like me."

"He pays women for sex." I say it like it changes something, when it clearly doesn't.

"Money, food, a roof over their head—a lot of people trade stuff for sex." There's accusation in his eyes.

Please someone get me the fuck out of this goddamn place.

I notice how red his eyes are, which means he's more than likely stoned and know having any form of argument with him is a lost cause. I sigh, giving up, and back toward the door. "Fine, I'll just hitchhike a ride." I both love and hate the idea of doing this. Love it because of the thrill. And hate it because I love doing things like this—love the danger because it's all I have left anymore. Risks. Well, really they're not risks anymore because what do I have to lose?

Preston rolls his eyes. "Don't be overdramatic. I'll drive you to school, but you're on your own for the day because I have shit to do."

19

Finding my own ride anywhere else means probably hitchhiking, since I don't have any friends, except for maybe Greyson, who I still talk to at work and hang out with sometimes, but I don't think he has any classes today and I hate asking people for favors—it's bad enough I have to ask Preston.

"Sounds like a plan to me." I force a chipper tone as I turn for the door, ready to get the day over with.

The last month has been really intense, especially with my parents' case being highly investigated due to Luke coming forward and giving them information about Mira Price, his mom. I haven't talked to Luke about it because I can barely look at him as it is without feeling both agony and something else that I don't think I've felt before. The case still hasn't gone anywhere. Mira Price has been questioned and detective Stephner, who's in charge of the investigation, is trying to get enough evidence to get a search warrant for her house. When I asked why Luke and I couldn't just testify, he said he wasn't sure if a song would hold up in court—they needed more. DNA proof or something better. I wonder what the hell would be left in her house after all these years—I'm sure she's destroyed any evidence—so I'm pessimistic at the idea that an arrest will ever be made.

However, what the case has done is spark tons of media attention, which has made my life a living hell. People like Stan, the reporter who harassed me through phone calls, pop up left and right. It's nerve-racking, especially because any of the texts could be from the real killer since there are two people out in the world that did it and they could still be lingering around, watching me.

What if he finally comes looking for me?

During one brief, semi-intoxicated meltdown, I told Preston my fears about this, which led to me stupidly divulging more than what I intended, like what went on between Luke and I, which he uses against me. So not only am I constantly looking over my shoulder, but I have Preston reminding me of what I'll have left if I leave him—absolutely nothing. Still, sometimes I want to take the nothing.

I try not to think too much about it, though, as I head out the front door with Preston close behind me. When I reach Preston's old grey Cadillac parked in the driveway, he steps around and opens the door, holding it open like a true gentleman, but he's not. Something that he proves to me with his next move, when I veer around him to get in the car and he grabs my hip and pulls me against him.

I picture myself standing on top of the tallest building and soaring off of it with my arms spanned to my side as he presses himself up against me and kisses the back of my head.

"I was thinking that maybe tomorrow we could do something fun for your birthday," he says, his fingers wandering downward toward my lower hipbone and pins and needles stab at my skin.

"My birthday was over a month ago," I say flatly. *Shut down. Shut down.* "And honestly I don't want to celebrate the day I came into this world."

"God, what the hell is wrong with you? You're always so down all the time." He dips his lips to my ear and nibbles at my lobe. "Don't I do everything for you... give you everything you want?" His fingers slip underneath the waistband of my pants and brushes my skin. "Let me do something special for you or better yet, let's do something together."

"I'm not in the mood to sit around and get high while you cop a feel." I want to run. Take off down the road and never stop. Outrun what I'm feeling inside. The confusion. The disgust over this and the last couple of months. The obligation, something I know Preston will remind me of if I tell him to quit touching me.

His fingers dig into my skin, his flirty mood shifting to anger—I've said the wrong thing again. "Why can't you be more grateful? Jesus, sometimes I think it might be best if I just kick you out. Just let you go live on the street. You could be a whore and make money that way."

"Maybe I should." I bite down on my lip as soon as I say it because I don't want to be homeless right now, not with everything else going on. "Fine, if you want to do something for my birthday, we can." I attempt to clean up the mess I made while I concentrate on picturing what it would be like to come to the end of the fall and crash. Would it feel like I was flying for a moment? Or would I just fall? Would I feel the pain when I hit the ground? My bones breaking. Or would I blackout before I even made it there?

"Good girl," he says. "You're always so good at doing what you're told." Then he kisses my neck, sucking on it before pulling away and my heart accelerates rapidly, but I remain dead on the outside and let the images of me splattered on the ground completely consume me, but then they shift into something else, which happens sometimes. My mind goes from being on that ledge to falling into Luke's arms.

Safe.

It would be so much easier if that feeling had stayed, but I know all too well that nothing good ever does.

Chapter 2

Luke

There are always two things on my mind—booze and money. Or booze and gambling. It's all I can focus on because the moment I stop and I let my mind catch up with life is the moment I think of *her*. Violet Hayes. The one girl who wrecked me in what I once thought was a the best kind of way possible when she broke me down, made me only think about her—made me want only her. But then it was taken away. Or stolen away by what my mother did. I should have known that I couldn't escape my past—that leaving to go to college wasn't enough to get away from the madness that is my mother. That she would find a way to have control over my life, like she used to when I was a kid. I should have known it wasn't over yet.

After Violet moved out of the apartment two months ago, I called the police and reported what facts I knew about the murders. It was only a little bit, but I knew I owed Violet at least that much. But the phone call hasn't led to much, unfortunately. The police haven't found any real hard evidence to arrest my mother, but they're trying to and I keep my fingers crossed everyday that something will happen.

I think part of me hoped that by telling the police, Violet would come back to me. But she didn't. And the more time goes by, the less I think she ever will. If I was stronger, I'd go to my mother's house and search for evidence myself, even though I have no idea where anything would be. But I wonder, what could be hiding in the chaos. That perfect, clean house upstairs, covers up the years of crap she's held onto that's piled up in the basement. But the idea of going there and seeing that woman…feeling that kind of rage… it makes me afraid of what I might do to her. So the wall remains between Violet and I, building higher and higher with each moment while I die a little bit more.

To help wake up every morning, I try to tell myself that I'll get over Violet eventually, because time is supposed to heal all wounds or some stupid shit like that, but it seems like time is having the opposite effect on me. The wounds have become infected and they're seeping through my body and rotting me from the inside out. To add to the crap going on, I got a copy of my sister, Amy's, journal she had before she committed suicide when she was sixteen-years-old. I didn't ask for the journal, but my mother found it in one of her boxes and randomly sent it to me, playing her usual mind games, trying to tear me open by reminding me of my sister's death.

"Remember how your sister left me," my mother had said when I'd called her up after I'd gotten the journal in the mail, wondering what the fuck it was. "You need to come back to me, Lukey. Don't leave me—don't be Amy."

"Go to hell!" I'd yelled and hung up on her, feeling a fire so potent in my chest, I ended up tearing apart my room just to settle down.

I wasn't planning on reading the journal because nothing that came from my mother has ever led to anything good. However, with too much free time on my hands the damn thing started haunting me and I finally cracked. The first thing I discovered was there was no way my mother even took the time to read it before she sent it to me and she should have. The stuff on the pages paints a horrible, very true picture of the kind of sick, messed up person my mother is. Whenever I read a page or two, I learn more and more about how much stuff was going on between Amy and my mother that I didn't understand while living with them. For example, the time my mother tried to whore Amy out to one of her drug dealers for payment…

Twelve years old and my mother is asking me to do something that sounds so wrong at my age. To be with a guy… like that… I don't know what to do. But she says it'll help pay the bills and other stuff. I'm not sure what the other stuff is but I'm guessing it has to do with that shit she keeps making my brother inject in her veins, which I know

*isn't diabetic medicine like my mother keeps telling me.
I'm not stupid. I know she's doing drugs.*

*But I wonder, if I can sleep with this guy she owes
money to… give up my virginity to save the family from getting kicked out on the streets, if my mother will finally say
thank you to me for helping out and that maybe, just maybe
she'll tell me she loves me.*

Each word I read makes my hatred for my mother
grow and the rage in my chest expand. Pretty soon, I'm going to be filled with so much hate, I'm going to drown in it.
So I do the only thing I can do to cope with it. I drown myself in other stuff, just like I do to hide the pain connected
to losing Violet.

I drown myself in other stuff, just like I do to conceal
the pain connected to losing Violet.

For the last couple of months, my nights have been
filled with booze, gambling, partying, and fights, some of
which I go looking for and others are thrown at me like
when I get caught cheating during a game. I know I should
stop, not because it's unhealthy--I'm a diabetic—but one of
these days I'm going to piss off the wrong person or take
one too many drinks. But I just can't find it in me to give a
shit. Live or die. It's all the same to me anymore.

Sleep's become a foreign concept, along with eating
and drinking anything that doesn't come in liquid form and

gives me an after burn that numbs my heart, soul, and mind. When I do manage to close my eyes, my past haunts me. It's becoming impossible to escape, so I try not to sleep as much as I can. I think it's starting to show, at least that's what I wonder when I walk out into the living room this morning.

Seth's sitting on the sofa when I walk in, yawning and dreary-eyed from no sleep. He glances up from the laptop with a disgusted look on his face as he takes in the sight of me. "No offense man, but you look like shit," he says, closing the computer as he takes in my sunken eyes and the healing bruise on my cheek, remnants of last weekends fight after I was accused of cheating down at Denny's. Thankfully, the guys that hang there are a bunch of pussies and I got away with minimal scratches and quite of few swings myself. Unfortunately I can't go back there anymore to gamble so I'm going to have to find somewhere else to make some cash.

"Shut the fuck up," I grumble back at Seth, running my hand over my messy brown hair. It's getting sort of scraggily since I haven't had a haircut in a while. But I haven't cared enough to go.

Seth flips me off, then rolls his eyes. "You need to get over this shit. Seriously. It's going to kill you."

"Get over what?" I play dumb.

He rolls his eyes again. "I'd tell you but I don't dare say her name because you'll give me that wounded Bambi look and then rip my head off."

"I'm not a wounded Bambi," I snap harshly and then swallow the lump forming in my throat. I snatch my jacket off the counter, before going over to the fridge. "Where the hell did the bottle of Jack Daniels go? And the Vodka?" I ask.

Seth puts his laptop aside, stands up from the sofa, and walks over to the counter area. "You finished it off last night before you went out to wherever it is you go." He pauses like he's waiting for me to tell him, but I don't because I can barely remember what I did five minutes ago, let alone five hours ago.

I slam the fridge door and open the cupboard next to it where Greyson, Seth's boyfriend, and my friend and roommate, keeps his stash of Cherry Vodka. "You think he'll mind if I drink some of this?" I ask Seth, reaching for the bottle which is only about a quarter of the way full.

Seth shrugs as he leans against the counter. "I don't think he'll mind that some is gone since he barely drinks." He wavers. "But I think he'll mind that *you're* drinking."

I grab the bottle, wanting—*needing*—to get some in my system. I'm starting to shake just thinking about it—starting to think way too fucking much. "I always drink."

"Yeah, but..." he trails off, massaging the back of his neck tensely.

I scowl at him. "But what? Just finish whatever it is you're going to say."

He sighs, letting his arm drop to his side. "Look, I get the whole drinking thing. I do it myself a hell of a lot, but Greyson and I have been talking and it seems like..." He shifts his weight, appearing uncomfortable. "You've been doing it more lately, particularly in the last month or so."

"You mean since Violet left." I ignore the knife slashing at my chest and it's easier with the vodka in my hand.

He reluctantly nods. "Yeah, pretty much." He blows out a breath, tugging his fingers through his blond hair. "Look I don't know what happened between you and Vio..." He trails off when he catches sight of my expression. "Her. But it's obvious that you're having a hard time dealing with it and you might... You might want to think about taking it easy on the shots and whatever the hell it is that you do all night." He gives a pressing look at my unwashed jeans and my wrinkled plaid shirt, then at my face. "It's starting to show. Seriously, you looking like the walk-

31

ing dead all the time. I don't even know how the hell you manage to go to school. And what about football practice? Doesn't the season start in a couple of weeks? Shouldn't you be getting in shape or whatever the hell you athletic types do to get ready for game season?"

He's telling me things I already know and that I don't care about, so I disregard him and start to unscrew the cap off the vodka. "I'm fine. I don't do anything I can't handle. And I work out all the time." Lie. I've been slacking, something my best friend Kayden noted the other day when I didn't show up for workouts. But not enough that I've lost a lot of muscle tone or anything and I honestly have a hard time finding the will to go, which is strange for me. My normal need for structure and order all fucked up, the only thing on track at the moment is school.

Seth shakes his head. "That's the biggest bunch of shit I've ever heard come out of your mouth. You're not fine— nothing is fine with you anymore. In fact, I think you're about two seconds away from falling apart."

I tip my head back to take a swig, the burning liquid instantly coating my mouth and I feel twenty times better. I take a long gulp, ignoring the bland cherry flavor, then lower the bottle from my mouth. "Since when did you become so concerned about my life?" I wipe my lips with the back of my hand.

He shakes his head, disappointed by something. "Since you obviously stopped caring about yourself."

I drop the bottle of Vodka into my bag, swing the handle over my shoulder, and brush by him, heading for the front door. "I care about my life." *Lie.* "Otherwise I wouldn't get up every day and go to class." Another lie. The only reason I do is a) because I have a weird issue with needing structure and school is the only thing that gives it to me anymore and b) It's the only place I get to see Violet—seeing her consistently for the last week has been worth the pain in the ass of getting up to go. And even though it hurts like a motherfucker every time I see her, I must enjoy self-inflicting pain because I still want to see her.

Seth opens his mouth to argue, but I turn away from him and walk out the door. Luckily school's within walking distance otherwise I'd have to ask Seth for a ride. It's a decent day and I attempt to focus on that fact as I make the way to school. But then I hear my phone ring from inside my pocket, a familiar tune, and the possibility of having a good day diminishes. Even though I don't want to answer it and talk to her, I want to hear what she has to say—I always do—but only because I hope that she'll finally let something slip that will help the investigation lead to her arrest.

33

"What do you want?" I snap into the receiver after three rings as I stumble up the sidewalk.

"Hey Luke," my mom singsongs, either delusional or high—it's hard to tell anymore. "How's my little boy doing?"

"I'm not your little boy." I make my way across the street, stumbling over the curb in the process. "So stop calling me that."

"Oh, you'll always be my little boy," she replies as I approach the other side of the street and then start down the sidewalk. "When are you coming home?"

Rage burns inside me, a violent fire in my chest, as I think about everything she's ever done to me in that hellhole she calls home. How she's always acted like it meant nothing—that everything she did to me and to my sister meant nothing. How she managed to ruin my life even when I wasn't living at home. How she might have killed someone, or at least been a part of it. All the harm she's done. All the lives she's ruined.

"I'm never fucking coming home," I say venomously, causing a guy walking down the street to sidestep and put space between us, like I'm the crazy one. "I have a life now. Here. Away from you and everything you did and do."

"What's that supposed to mean?" She sounds hurt, just like the day she called me up and asked me why I'd told the police she might have been part of a murder that happened almost fourteen years ago. I told her the truth, that I knew what she did and called them. She denied everything; the song, the night where she came home with blood on her clothes, even though I saw her. And by our next phone call, she was already denying I'd told the police anything. Like she thinks if she pretends it didn't happened then it didn't. But it did. She ruined a life. She stole lives. She did things that she needs to pay for and that I'll always pay for being her child.

"You know what it means," I say. "So stop playing stupid."

"No I don't," she lies. Or maybe she's not lying. Or this is all a game to her. Maybe she's ill. Needs help. I honestly don't know but I've wondered it most of my life. If perhaps there's something wrong with her head. Regardless, she needs to be locked up somewhere, where she can't hurt anyone.

"Have you talked to the police lately?" I cut across the lawn in front of someone's house and ungracefully hop the fence, taking a short cut down a narrow alley.

"No, not since that night I called you about a week ago... why?"

"Just wondering if you were still in trouble," I tell her flatly, grabbing onto a fence when I get a killer head rush and the world starts to spin. "Or if you finally admitted what you did."

"I was never in trouble. They told me they had the wrong person and that it was all over and that the person that called was never going to call again." She pauses. "Lukey, please come home. I'm lonely. Remember how Amy left me—left us. I need you. Don't be like her—don't leave me."

"I'm not coming home ever." When I reach the end of the alley, I jog across the street to the campus yard, filled with trees, green grass, and people going to and from the parking lot.

"You have to," she whines. "I can't take this empty house anymore... being alone... it makes me think about doing bad things."

I pause on the sidewalk right before I step onto the grass, fear and anger blasting through me that she's doing this again. "Knock that shit off, Mother."

"You need to come home before something bad happens."

I hate her even more. I didn't think it was possible, but apparently it is, feeling the anger simmering inside me, possessing me. "I'm never coming home. That's where all the bad shit happens!"

"Yes, you are! You are!" She starts to sob hysterically and with each sob my hatred for her expands and I become even angrier until I'm drowning in it, struggling to get above the red blinding me. Finally I can't take it anymore and hang up on her. But the rage still singes under my skin, simmering, festering, killing me.

I take a deep breath then another and finally reach for my bag to take out the Vodka. I chug the remainder of it, knowing I'm going to push my body to the brim of being able to function, but I need the numbness more than I need air. I need to erase this hatred stirring inside me.

After I finish it off, I discard the empty bottle into a nearby garbage can and cut across the campus yard, bumping people out of my way, sometimes accidentally and sometimes intentionally, but none of them utter a word to me. By the time I arrive at the edge of the main entrance of the campus, the trees and brick buildings are starting to become blurry and all I can see is red. Anger. Red. Hatred. More anger. I seriously almost turn around and walk back home, deciding I've overdone it and it'd probably be best to just go back and let myself pass out. Then I see something that stops me dead in my tracks. A beat up grey Cadillac pulling up at the curb just in front of the main building.

Violet.

It'd be okay—in fact I'd welcome it—except for the fact that Preston the fucking asshole is dropping her off. The guy's a creepy pervert, who sells drugs and also has Violet selling drugs for him. Not to mention he's hit her before. I still can't believe she went back to him when she took off. Just thinking of them under the same roof makes my skin crawl like it's full of infected wounds. I tried to get a hold of her when I found out she'd moved back in with him, but she would never answer her phone or return my messages. When I finally did see her again on the first day of classes, she pretended like I didn't exist and it's been that way every damn day.

I stop near the trees and watch her as she climbs out of the car. She's wearing tight black pants, a vest, and a purple shirt that's just short enough that I can see a speck of her side that I know is covered with a tattoo, patterns of curves and flowers inking up her ribcage. Her black and red hair is down and I can't help but remember the few times where I ran my fingers through it and pulled on it as she moaned in response.

God, the way she moaned was incredible. What I'd give to hear it again. Touch her again... my fingers ache just thinking about it. But instead I'm stuck watching her at a distance as she shuts the car door and turns for the entrance of the school. Then Preston gets out for some reason and when he says something to her, she pauses, halting near the edge of the sidewalk. She doesn't turn around, just staring straight ahead at the brick building as he winds around the back of the car and toward her. If I didn't know any better I'd think they were a couple, by the way he moves up behind her, puts his hands on her hips, and leans over her shoulder, getting close and pressing his body against hers.

I see a bright flash of red. Feel the fire in my chest ignite and ignite through every part of my body. I want to walk over there and slam my fist into his face repeatedly, see how badly I can hurt him, especially when he whispers something in her ear. Then he adds fuel to the fire scorching violently inside me when he takes his hand and stuffs it into Violet's back pocket, either touching her or putting something in there. Either way, it's annoying and the compulsion to go over there and tell him she's mine nearly devours me. Still, I'm too drunk and am losing control of my thoughts and actions. I take a step toward them and another, stepping out of the shadows of the trees—God knows what I'm going to do—but then I come to a cold stop as Violet turns around and lets Preston lean in and kiss her.

The redness in my vision dissipates. Everything around me goes out of focus and nothing makes sense anymore. I feel cold inside and I wonder if I've died. I painfully realize that over the last month, while I've been hung up on Violet and what we had, she's moved on. Moved forward. While I've been stuck in the past, unable to escape it no matter what I do.

Violet

I can't believe what just happened. Preston kissed me in public. Of all the places he could have done it. It's one thing for him to do it in the house, where I can shut my eyes and fall into myself, but out in the open, in front of people, it feels too real. So warped and wrong. Makes me feel so disgusting.

I wanted to jerk back, but when he put enough weed into my pocket that if I get caught I'm probably going to be screwed, then proceeded to tell me that I needed to sell it by the end of the day or else I'm out of the house, I remembered everything I'd lose. I know it's not much, but it's all I have at the moment.

After he drives away, I stand there, weak and pitiful, hating myself for it. By the time I reach the door of my first class of the day, I'm stewing in all sorts of emotions and have the most overpowering urge to turn away from the classroom door, bail out on class, and instead go find something reckless to do. The problem is I never miss class. It's my one goal in life—my only accomplishment.

As I'm heading into the classroom, I'm a little distracted, and react slowly as someone enters the doorway at the same time. Our shoulders collide and I shuffle back, angry Violet rising and ready to take it out on someone.

"Where'd you learn how to walk?" I say coldly. The second I say it though I catch the scent of Vodka, cigarettes, and cologne; a scent that I'm very familiar with. I glance up and am greeted by a pair of intense brown eyes, an unshaven jawline, scraggily brown hair, and a pained expression that I'm sure matches my own. "Luke." I don't mean to say it aloud but it slips out. He looks terrible up close, a bruised cheek, and dark circles under his eyes, exhausted. A gnawing feeling forms in my gut as I wonder if it's my fault he looks this way. I want to ask him what happened, but emotions slam through me, filled with invisible razors, needles so potent and painful I can barely breathe. I want to touch him so badly. Kiss him. Feel his tongue slip against mine. I desperately want everything we had a couple of months ago. The smiles. The rainbows. The sunshine and even the ridiculous cheesiness of the dates and flirting even though normally I couldn't stand it. But with Luke things were different. I'd more than welcome it all right now if it meant it could get rid of how I've been feeling.

But it can't—nothing can erase the past and just being near him reminds me of my parents. And how I ran from him because of that and what I did with Preston.

I should move away from him, yet I can't bring myself to do so, finally feeling alive for the first time in two months. I hate to admit it, but it's true. I've been a walking zombie, a hollow shell, like I was for so many years, but not at this moment. And apparently neither can he. So we end up standing there, staring at each other, stuck some-where between reality and the make believe land we wished existed; the one where monsters never showed up at night at my house and his mother wasn't one of them. The one where we could touch each other and not have to think. The one where we could be together and not hurt. The one we had before we found out the truth.

It's the first time we've been this close since the truth was discovered and it's more powerful and potent than I ever imagined. We don't speak, move, breathe, even when people file in and out of the classroom doorway between us. Our eyes are locked, our breaths ragged. The longer we stare at each other, the more confused he looks and the more lost I feel because I'm not moving away. Instead I feel like I'm being pulled toward him, or maybe it's more that I'm falling. I'm not sure. And I don't want to be sure. What I want is for time to stand still, right at this moment, so we never have to move forward again.

But then his lips part, and everything around me unfreezes. I have no idea what's going to come out of his mouth. If I'll hate it. Like it. Want it—maybe. And maybe I'll take it.

I never get to find out, though, because the professor walks between us and breaks the moment like glass, the sharp pieces exploding and scattering around us. We're both abruptly reminded that make believe is just that and doesn't really exists unless you live in a fairytale.

Chapter 3

Luke

I'm bailing out on school. I can't take it today, walking around in the same building, seeing her, wanting to touch her, kiss her, fuck her, do whatever I want with her. We were so close and all that desire and need was ripping through me, even though I'd just seen her kiss another guy five minutes ago. I wanted her more than anything. Right there in the hallway, in front of everyone. And I was drunk enough to try it. But then the professor walked by and broke our little moment. And I swear to God, it broke me as well.

I sit in the back row and watch her take notes the entire length of class and it's pure torture. Finally, I decide that I need to get the hell out of here, so instead of heading to my next class, I leave the campus. I think about calling my best friend, Kayden Owens, and seeing what he's up to, but I don't really feel like having company. I feel like doing something that will distract me. Something reckless. Dangerous. Something that comes with risks, chances for trouble, fighting.

I go back to my apartment and grab my stash of cash, which I keep in my sock drawer. I have three thousand bucks and start counting out half of it, but then take the whole damn thing with me. I stuff the stash into my pocket and then head out the door, pausing when I see that I forgot to put the copy of Amy's journal away. It's opened up to the page I'd randomly turned to last night; the one where she starts to get depressed, right after Caleb raped her. If only we would have found this sooner, then maybe she could have gotten some help.

I can't live like this anymore. I can't feel this way. I just want to feel like a normal person again, not so sick and wrong on the inside. I want to feel like Amy again.

I shut the notebook and tuck it under the pillow, the thought haunting my mind as I stagger drunkenly out of the apartment and toward the condos on 5th and Grove, knowing that despite the warm and welcoming appearance of the area, I'm going to a very dangerous place. I've heard stories about where I'm going, the things the guys are involved in, the consequences that come with screwing them over. But I don't have the will to give a shit.

As I'm heading for the entrance door, my phone starts ringing inside my pocket and Kayden's name flashes across the screen. I know if I answer it, he's going to ask me why I missed class and if I'm coming to work out. When I say no, he's going to start questioning me and I had enough questions from Seth this morning. So I send him to voicemail and finish the journey to the door. Before I enter the lobby,

I give Toverson, the guy who invited me to a game here a couple of weeks ago, a shout on the phone.

He answers after four rings. "What's up?"

"Hey, it's Luke." I shield my eyes from the sun with my hand as I lean against the entrance door. "I think I want to take you up on your offer and sit in on a game."

"Where are you at?" he asks. I can hear voices in the background, sounds of poker chips clinking together, and loud music. I crave to be there, crave the solitude it'll give me like fucking women used to do before I met Violet.

"I'm actually downstairs, just outside the lobby." I glance through the door at the security person sitting behind the desk, watching me like a hawk.

"You know about the high buy in, right?" he asks, the noise in the background fading. "It's more than just the hundred like it is at Denny's."

"Yeah, I know. I brought three thousand with me."

He pauses and seconds later I hear a door shut. The background noises go completely quiet. "No offense, but where'd you get that sort of cash?"

"I've been saving up." I don't bother telling him it's all I have, since it's none of his business.

"All right then, I'll buzz you up," he says but then pauses. "But just a little bit of warning. These guys up here don't mess around like they do at Denny's so be careful. You get caught doing anything they don't like and they won't just let you off with a slap on the hand."

"I got it," I say. He's subtly warning me—don't cheat or else you're fucked.

I always cheat though and I have no plans of stopping now. It takes the thrill out of it and I need the thrill. Still, I dither for a moment, the alcohol in my system settling just enough for me to see through the haze and I almost chicken out. The feeling only amplifies when I see a guy three times my size open the door and greet me. But then the alcohol starts scorching through my veins again and I follow him inside and up to the second floor. When he opens the door and lets me in, I feel so much better. Tables, black, red, white, and blue chips. The smoke. The booze. Women everywhere. Danger. Risks. Suddenly I feel very content inside. All of my distractions—my addictions— are right in front of me and I want them all.

Violet

School drags by slower than usual. Maybe that's because of my encounter with Luke. Or maybe it's just because I know I'm going fishing when it's over—fishing for a guy, who knows a lot of guys, who like to get high. I'd been upset at first when Preston asked me to do this on a Monday, but I decided after my spazz out with Luke, that maybe I needed a break from the reality of being stuck in my own head. Perhaps I needed to be that girl again who dressed up, played the part, and didn't give a shit about anyone or anything.

After my last class, I find the bathroom and slip into the outfit I keep in my bag for occasions like these. A short black dress that shows off my legs and I top the outfit off with red lipstick and glittery high heels. I look like a prostitute but that's kind of the point. Seduction. I'm going to go through with it. I'm going to be *that* girl again.

I can do this," I mutter to my reflection as I look in the mirror. But the girl in the mirror looks unconvinced. Taking a quick break, I turn away and lean against the sink to make a phone call I try to make at least once a week.

"Hello, Detective Stephner speaking," he answers after two rings.

"This is Violet," I say, shutting my eyes and crossing my fingers that maybe this will be the time he gives me good news. "Violet Hayes. I was just… checking in."

As soon as he sighs, I know nothing has changed. "Violet, I know you want to know—and trust me we do to—but these things take time."

"It's been almost two months."

"I know. We're still working on getting the search warrant approved."

"Can't you move any faster?" I say more harshly than I planned. "Sorry, it's just that it's driving me crazy."

"I know," he replies. "And trust me, I'm not resting until it's solved either. But I also need you to let me call you when something happens, instead of checking in all the time."

"Sorry for bugging you," I mutter, opening my eyes.

"You're not bugging me at all. I just want you to stop stressing about this and try to live a normal life," he says. "And while we're on the phone, how's the texting from that reporter? Did he stop?"

"Yeah, he did." I stand up straight and collect my bag from the floor. "Thanks for getting that restraining order put on him."

"Anytime." There's another pause and I know what's coming before he says it. "What about Mira Price's son?

Have you talked to him at all since I brought him in for questioning?"

"Not really." My chest starts to tighten, my lungs constricting and sucking away the air. *Stop it. Turn it off.*

"I think that's for the better," he says. "At least for now."

I get what he's saying, but it feels so wrong. For the better? If this is for the better, then why does it hurt so badly? "I have to go," I tell him. "It's time for my next class."

"Okay," he says. "And remember; call me if you need anything." But clearly he means call me only if you need something that doesn't have to do with checking in.

After I hang up, I pull myself together and walk out of the bathroom confidently, ready to move on from the conversation and go fishing—*the perfect distraction.* But the moment I step into the pond, I feel deflated, thinking about how much I'd rather be trying to drown myself instead of standing out in the campus yard, looking for a sucker. The longer I search the crowd, the more I just want to bail and deal with whatever punishment Preston's going to give me. I'm not feeling it and I'm about to give up when my phone buzzes from inside my pocket.

I take it out and unlock the screen. A text from an un-known number. Not surprising. It happens all the time anymore.

Unknown: I know what happened to your parents.

And let the games begin. I shake my head, thinking of Stan, and some of the other calls and texts I've gotten since the news went public. I consider what I should text back.

Me: Yeah, I think everyone does anymore u moron. They were murdered. Thanks for reminding me though. That was super-duper nice of you.

I start put my phone away but it buzzes in my hand. Sighing, I open the incoming message.

Unknown: But I know who did it.

I stop breathing as I read it over and over and for a brief, very gullible moment on my part I actually wonder if this person might really know something, like maybe about Mira or the other person that was there that night. But at the end of my analysis, I decide that it's probably just some god damn asshole, like Stan the reporter, and a few other one's I've sporadically met during my few trips to the po-lice station. I even received one phone call with someone bribing me with their information in exchange for a few gory details of what I saw that night. I wasn't stupid enough to believe that a reporter new more than the police and I do, so I told him where he could go fuck himself.

I'm about to text back and call the person out when I hear someone say, "Are you Violet?"

There's a guy standing in front of me and my entire body tenses as a million different thoughts race through my mind of who he could be. A reporter. The police. The other person who was there the night my parents were killed, although he looks too young for the latter.

He's wearing a fancy pinstripe shirt with the sleeves rolled up, along with a pair of name brand jeans, and shoes shinier than my lip-gloss. "You are Violet, right?"

Despite my alarm, I don't miss a beat, even though my heart does. "Why? What's it to you?"

His lips spread to a slow smile as he sticks out his hand for me to shake. "I'm Roy. Preston told me I could probably find you down here and that you could hook me and some of my colleagues up."

"He did, huh?" I say, relaxing. Preston knows my routine a little too well, I guess. Still I don't appreciate the unannounced ambush. "Yeah, I'm her."

His smile broadens, but his brows furrow when I won't shake his hand. "Good, come with me."

I don't budge from my spot underneath the tree. "Yeah, I'm going to need to check with Preston before I go anywhere with some random dude who looks like he could be a lawyer and who could be setting me up."

His smile falters, but then he relaxes and bobs his head up and down. "Yeah. Totally. I understand."

"Give me a second." I wander away from him, dialing Preston's number when I reach out-of-hearing range.

"Hey beautiful." Preston sounds like he might be high and having a party with all the background noise. "I was expecting your call."

"Why? Because you sent some rich douche down here without telling me?" I say, glancing back at Roy who has his attention focused on a girl in a skirt bending over to pick up a paper she dropped and who's totally flashing the entire campus yard.

"I was testing you," he explains simply. "I want to make sure we don't have anymore screw ups in our future."

I roll my eyes. "So did I pass or fail?"

"You passed," he says and I can hear the grin in his voice. "Which means only good punishments for you to-night."

My heart withers a little more—soon there won't be anything left of it. "If it's okay with you, and your test is over, I'll get back to fishing."

"No, Violet, you need to go with Roy." He talks loudly over the music.

I press my finger to my ear so I can hear better. "Why? I thought it was a test?"

"A test yeah, but Roy has a connection to this underground poker game place in one of the more upper ends of Laramie and if we can impress him he might just make us his permanent dealers, which is a good thing. Trust me. We're getting in with the big timers."

I try not to freeze up at the mention of underground poker games, because I know Luke likes to hangout at those kinds of places and big timers are a lot different than dumbass college guys who think with their dicks. "I'm not sure I want to do this deal."

"Violet, don't fuck this up for me," he says, his anger rising through his voice. "This is a great opportunity and if you'll just act like your normal self, I know you can dazzle the shit out of them. Just make sure to give them *whatever* they want."

"I'm not a whore," I reply through gritted teeth, getting pissed. "I'm not going to fuck anyone."

"I never said you had to, but I think you have it in you, if you had to," he says. I'm about to yell at him, right in front of Roy when he adds, "Look, I'm sure no one expects you to fuck them or give them a blowjob or anything. Just smile and show them your cleavage and I'm sure my product will seal the deal. You can save the fucking and blowjobs for me later. In fact, I'd kind of prefer it if you did."

I squeeze my eyes closed and tell myself to shut it all down. *Don't feel a thing.* "Fine, I'll do it, but I swear to God if someone says something about you saying that I was going to take care of them, I'll kick you in the balls when I get home."

"I like it when you talk kinky to me," he says with a deep chuckle. "Now get out there and make me happy then come back to me. I'm starting to miss you."

I feel like I'm going to barf right here all over the grass in front of everyone. I shake my head, annoyed, but still tell him okay because I don't really have a choice. Then I hang up and go back over to Roy, smiling as sweetly as I can. "All right, Roy, where are we going?"

"Up on 5th and Grove," he says with a grin as his gaze lazily takes me in. We start across the campus yard. It's quiet between the two of us and I'm pretty content with it, but apparently, Roy isn't because he says, "So do you like playing Texas Hold'em?"

I shrug, trying not to think about the last time I played Texas Hold'em with Luke while he was wearing a towel. "It's okay, I guess."

He stops in front of a black Mercedes with tinted windows and shiny chrome trim. He aims the keys at it and it beeps, the lights flashing and the doors unlocking. "Well, if I were you, I'd pretend that you love it for tonight."

I nod, getting his meaning. "Got it."

We get into the car and he turns on the engine. Then he cranks the heat when he notices that I'm shivering a little from the chilly breeze outside. "You should have worn a jacket or something."

I glance down at the goosebumps on my legs. "A jacket isn't part of my uniform," I tell him, bouncing my knees up and down, trying to warm up.

"Oh, gottcha." He pushes the shifter into reverse. "There's some Vodka under the seat if you want a shot." He backs up the car and straightens the wheel, then flashes me a grin. "It might warm you up."

I'm about to decline because I'm not a fan of drinking—it makes me too crazy and emotional—but then I remember what I'm supposed to be. And that if I do mess this up, I mess up the little life that I have. So I put on my dazzling smile—the fake one I haven't worn in a while—then reach under the seat to take a shot, pretending to be okay. Pretending I'm not drowning in a sea of pain. Pretending that I'm okay with being here, when I'm not.

It used to be so much easier to do this, float around in life, detached from everyone, including myself. But that was before I met Luke and discovered what it was like to be happy. And the worst part of it is knowing I'll never have it again.

Chapter 4

Luke

I'm in deep shit but I'm still trying to figure out if I care. Some pop song plays from the surround sound, empty glasses cover the table, and I've doubled my money, mainly because I'm cheating and very carelessly, too. I should probably be more cautious, but I continue to ride high, drinking shot after shot with a curvy brunette on my lap. I've gotten everything I was looking for when I came here and I feel good for the most part, except for that goddamn spot in my heart that's screaming at me to stop. That there's something better than this out there for me. But what my fucking heart doesn't get is that she doesn't want me.

There are three other guys sitting at the table—Geraldson, the owner of the house, who is a big bulky dude, and the other two about the same height and weight as me, who are Carson and, I think, Dougford, who doesn't trust me. They're older and rougher than the usual crowd I play with. I think I even saw a gun tucked into the back of Geraldson's pants when I walked up to the table. Toverson is out on the back deck talking to someone on the cellphone, but keeps glancing through the door in my direction, giving me a look of warning.

"You in or out?" Carson asks, fanning through his chips as he tries to read my bluff.

I glance down at the eight of hearts and queen of spades in my hand and then at the four cards on the table; a five, seven, nine, and a jack. I'm about to fold, but then the brunette slants forward and presses her tits against my chin, giving me a face full of cleavage.

"Just go for it," she whispers in my ear, tickling her finger up and down the back of my neck. "It's so hot when guys are risky like that."

I'm about to tell her to fuck off, reach into my pocket and take out one of the cards I have hidden in there, but Dougford is watching my every move from across the table, so I toss the chips in, figuring I'll lose one hand to make my wins look more legit.

"I'm in." I say, being cocky for no goddamn reason.

Carson gives me an arrogant grin in return, but I think he's pretending he's got something when he doesn't. I relax back in the chair and grope the brunette's hips while the dealer flips over the river card. It's a two. Shit. I have absolutely nothing. Normally, I'd fold or switch my cards, but I remind myself to lose a hand and match the bet.

He grins like a prick as he lays his cards down and reveals that he has a pair of queens. It takes a lot not to shove the brunette off my lap, lean over and punch the grin off his face. I know the odds of his hand are pretty low, making me think that he might be cheating, so I decide no more cautious playing—I'm cheating with every hand that I can from now on.

To calm myself down, I pour myself another shot from the Tequila bottle on the table. I barely feel the burn anymore, barely feel anything at all.

It's Geraldson's turn to deal so he collects the cards while Dougford takes out a couple of cigars from a wooden box that's beside him. He smells one of them then gives Geraldson and Carson each one.

"You smoke?" he asks me in his raspy voice.

I shrug and take the cigar he's offering, figuring it might keep me content until I can step outside to have a smoke. People are so weird sometimes. No smoking cigarettes in the house, but cigars are perfectly okay?

I light up and inhale. It's not enough to soothe the hunger inside me, so I end up putting it out in the ashtray after three puffs.

"What? Not good enough for you?" Carson asks, separating his chips into color-coordinated piles.

I reach for the cards Gerard dealt me. "No, it's just not what I usually smoke." My tension starts to unravel when I see the ace in my hand. I've been waiting for the damn ace to show up so I could use the one I have up my sleeve. Pocket aces.

I'm trying not to grin as I get ready for the game to get going when the front door swings open and a guy around my age wearing preppy clothes and a cocky smile walks into the room.

"Roy, man. What's up?" Geraldson says, setting his cards face down on the table as he gets up from his chair to give the guy a one-handed hug.

"Not much," Roy says as he steps aside to let someone else in that's behind him. Suddenly, every single movement and noise around me fades.

Violet fucking Hayes.

She looks way too amazing, dressed in a short black dress that shows off her endless legs and the heels… goddamn what I would do to fuck her with just those heels on. I'm seriously getting a hard-on just thinking about it, which would be fine except the brunette on my lap must feel it pressing against her ass and she gets this look in her eyes like she thinks it's from her and is considering acting on it.

All of a sudden, I'm very aware that she's on my lap. Through the fogginess in my mind, I debate whether I care or not. Violet and I are over. I shouldn't care, but I do. I care so much that I hurry and push the brunette off my lap before Violet sees me.

However, I move too late and her eyes find me like magnets and I'm metal just as I'm shoving the woman off. There's a flash of jealousy in Violet's eyes as she glares at the woman who's gripping my shoulders to get her balance, and as disturbing as it is, I fucking love the sight of it in her eyes. That she still cares enough to get jealous.

What the fuck is wrong with me?

Violet tears her gaze off me as Roy says something to her and the woman that was on my lap gives me a nasty look before heading into the kitchen to get a drink. Violet sticks out her hand to shake Geraldson's hand, flashing him a fake smile—I know her well enough to know that's not her real smile. Geraldson doesn't stand a chance against whatever she's got up her sleeve—whatever the reason is that she's here. They say something to each other in low voices and I become very aware of why she's here. Dealing. Motherfucking hell, this isn't good. Not here with these guys. This isn't the same as her little deals with college frat boys. These are hardcore bookies and I'm guessing hardcore dealers.

"Sit. Have a drink and play with us," Geraldson says to Roy, gesturing at the table. Then he turns to Violet and arches his brow. "You like watching men play Texas Hold'em, sweet thing?"

She discreetly glances at me from the corner of her eye with a look on her face that I can tell means she's biting back a snide retort over Geraldson's sexist remark. "Sure," she says tightly.

"Good, then sit down, have a drink, and we'll chat." Geraldson grins and motions for her to sit down in an empty seat, the one beside me of all places. Violet looks tense, but still comes over and while she's walking, Geraldson's checking out her ass the entire way.

I expect Violet to waver before sitting, but being the pro that she is, she manages to take a seat without so much as a flash of hesitation. She doesn't look at me though, even when her leg brushes against mine from under the table, but it causes my breath to catch in my throat. *Guess I'm losing on the who wants who more hand.*

"Violet, this is Dougford, Carson," Gerald starts with introductions as he sits down at the table and then each guy reaches across the table to shake Violet's hand. Then he goes to me. "And this is Luke."

Violet turns her head in my direction, her eyes sparkling. If I didn't know better, I'd guess she was enjoying this. But how could she be when she can barely look at me in class?

"It's nice to meet you, Luke." She raises her eyebrows slightly then sticks out her hand for me to shake.

Okay, so I guess we're pretending like we don't know each other then. "And it's nice to meet you, Violet." I exhale as I take her hand and when our skin comes into contact, it's the first time in two months. I think I'm going deaf and blind, or maybe it's that she's taking over all of my senses. My thoughts are swirling so fast that my pulse starts to pound and between that and the amount of alcohol in me, I think I might blackout.

"Breathe." I swear to God she whispers this under her lips, but I'm not sure if it's to herself or me. Then she flinches, blinking her attention away from me, and calmly pulls her hand away from mine.

Roy goes over to the bar area and pours Violet a drink. Whiskey, I think by the amber liquid in the cup and then takes a seat himself. Violet casually gives the drink a sniff then takes a large swallow, forcing back a gag before setting the glass down on a coaster. She sits back without so much as a glance in my direction as the cards are dealt, talking to Geraldson about quantities and other shit that makes me so infuriated I get distracted and sloppier with each hand. I'm not being as careful as I should.

Get your act together. But it's difficult when she's chatting to a man with a gun tucked in the back of his pants about drugs.

"So, you think you'd want how much on a regular basis?" Violet asks Geraldson. I wonder if Violet's planning on screwing him over like she does with some of her clients. If so, I need to stop her. These are not the kind of people to be doing that to.

"An ounce to a quarter," Geraldson says as he studies the cards in his hand intently.

Violet's jaw tightens while I tense myself. It's a big amount, definitely not those little dime bags she usually deals. She quickly reaches for the glass of whiskey and finishes it off to hide her nervousness. I have to wonder if she even knows what she's getting into.

After a few large swallows, Violet sets the glass down on the coaster and collects herself. "Did you mention the amount to Preston?" she asks coolly.

Geraldson nods to her and then nods at the dealer to turn over the river card. "Yeah, he said you'd bring some samples with you today that we could test out."

Violets nod, appearing composed on the outside, but I know her better than that. She's uneasy—out of her element—as she reaches into her bra, pulls out a bag of weed, and tosses it onto the table on top of the chip pile.

"Nice," Roy says, eyeing her breasts and the weed while Dougford nods in agreement.

Geraldson sets his cards face down, picks up the bag, opens it up, and smells the inside of it with an approving look on his face. "Mind if I light a bowl?" he asks Violet. "Just to taste for quality?"

"That's what it's for," she replies, starting to fidget with her hands below the table.

Geraldson gets up to get a pipe and Violet glances around the room as if she's searching for an escape route. "Could one of you boys point me to the ladies' restroom?"

Nodding, Roy eagerly gets to his feet. "Yeah, let me show you." There's an excited look on his face, like a guy going to get a blowjob, as they walk out of the room together.

That stupid fire erupts inside my chest again and I'm unsure how to put it out. Or whether I even should.

Violet   ·

I want to bang my head against the wall. "Goddammit, Preston. That's too much weed to deal without some heavy consequences." It makes me wonder who the fuck these guys are exactly that they'd need that much weed. One of them is carrying a gun for hell's sake. Yeah, I'm a tough ass and have seen it all and it's not like I'm terrified. In fact, the danger adds adrenaline. But the idea of going to jail is not appealing, even for an adrenaline junkie.

After I get into the bathroom, blowing off Roy's remark of how perfect my mouth would look on his cock, I lock myself in and try to decide what to do. I want to bail, not just from this place, but from this lifestyle. How do I escape the only thing I know?

"Things were so much easier when I was with Luke," I mutter under my breath, grasping onto the edge of the bathroom counter as the truth nearly sends me to the floor. "Dammit, this is bad."

I rest my head against the mirror behind me, thinking about how Luke is here and how destiny is a real bitch, putting us together like this again. But deep down, I know it's not destiny. The probability of us ending up together like this, under the same roof, has always been high, since we both live the same risky lifestyles in the same damn town. I just wish the probability of us working out was higher.

"What the hell am I going to do?" I mumble.

Knock. Knock. Knock.

"Go away, Roy!" I shout, knowing I'm being unprofessional, but not caring at the moment. "I'm not giving you a blowjob."

There's a pause. "Violet, open up," Luke's voice floats through from the other side of the door. "It's me... Luke." Like he has to say his name—his damn gorgeous voice is branded into my mind for all eternity.

I raise my head up and scowl at the door. "Go away, Luke."

"No... Look, I get that you don't want to have anything to do with me—I really do—but you're in over your head here."

I inch over to the door and place my hand on it, closing my eyes and picturing him on the other side doing the same thing, even though I'm sure that's not true. I can see him in my mind, the most intense brown eyes I've ever seen. His lips that I know are the softest and gentlest I've ever kissed. His lean arms that made me feel safe once. And it's okay for me to picture this as long as we have a barrier between us, like this door.

"You don't think I know that? I know I'm in deep shit. Trust me. I knew it the moment I walked in."

It takes a second for him to answer. "I think you might think you know that, but you're not walking away so... I want to help you."

"I don't want your help." I open my eyes when he doesn't respond and reach for the doorknob, figuring he did what I asked and decided to leave me alone, since he's been good about giving me space. But when I open the door, he's still standing on the other side and he comes barreling in without warning, forcing me back into the bathroom and then slamming the door behind us and locking it.

He's panting, as if he's all worked up as he leans back against the door and just stares at me in the most unnerving way that makes me all fidgety. There's too little space between us... too little breathing room... I need to breathe... I need to rip his clothes off... I think the whiskey I drank earlier has burnt away my rationality. I shake the last thought from my head.

"What do you want?" I finally ask in a clipped tone, crossing my arms and refusing to look away from him, even though I desperately want to. "Why are you looking at me like that?"

He gives his head a little shake, muttering something under his breath before standing up straight. "Why are you here?"

I gape at him. "I was here first. You're the one that followed me back here and then forced your way in here."

He dithers then takes a tentative step toward me, forcing me to take a step back toward the towel rack. "I mean, here, at Geraldson's house?" he asks. "You don't want to be messing around with these people, Violet." He glances at the shut door then his concerned gaze lands back on me. "This isn't the same as those frat guys you fuck over."

"You don't think I know that?" I hiss. "But I don't have a choice, do I? I live with Preston and this is how I pay him for that."

"Pay him?" He lets out a flabbergasted laugh as he spans his hands to the side and takes another step toward me, slightly unstable on his feet, which means he's probably drunk. "The guy is a fucking asshole. You don't owe him anything... you shouldn't even be with him."

I take a step back and then another until I'm bumping into the wall and the towel rack is pressed against my side. I have nowhere else to go besides the shower or out the window. Being in the confined space with whiskey soaring in my system is making the air buzz electrically and my brain foggy. *I need to get out... but I kind of don't want to.*

"Well, I don't really have a choice, do I?" I say. "Since I have nowhere else to live at the moment besides the streets."

His face drains of color and then he reaches out to touch me, as if to soothe me, but I lean my head away as far as it will go. He freezes, appearing horrified. "Why are you so afraid of me?" he asks, his hand lifelessly falling to his side. "I would never hurt you. Not on purpose anyway."

"I know you wouldn't, but it still hurts." We're talking in code and I want to cry, but I make those damn traitor tears stay in my eyes. I never cry. Only once, when I found out about Luke's mother and I promised myself never again—I'm stronger than that. "And besides, I'm afraid of myself being near you, not the other way around." And I'd like to thank the booze for the last comment.

He swallows hard. "I'm sorry." His voice is barely audible, so much agony emitting from his eyes that it submerges me. He looks just like I feel and I want to make both of us feel better.

I'm not even sure what overcomes me, if it's him, me, the powerful, lustful emotions blazing between us, the need to rip his clothes off, or the alcohol searing my veins; but I find myself stepping toward him. I haven't forgotten or moved past what happened, but I let myself stop caring for a brief second, letting my walls down just enough that I can put my hand on his chest.

He sucks in I sharp breathe from the contact, his heart rate instantly quickening beneath my palm. "Fuck," he utters and then he's leaning forward. I think he's going to kiss me, but instead he just rests his forehead against mine. He breathes raggedly, in and out, in and out, his solid chest crashing into my breasts.

I wait for him to touch me, but he doesn't. Wait for him to do *something*, but he doesn't. He's motionless, like he's giving me the chance to leave. I should. Just walk around him and go out the door. Never look back. But having him this close to me causes intense memories to flood my body, reminds me that being touched by a guy doesn't have to feel wrong or dirty. That it can feel right. It did once with Luke and I selfishly want it again.

Suppressed emotions, alcohol and a hunger I've never felt before possess me and suddenly I'm crashing my lips against his. He sucks in a startled breath, slanting back slightly, as if to pull away, but then in a snap of a finger, he's grabbing me by the hips and yanking me against him as he seals his mouth to mine. The heat of him… the taste of him… it's so potent… so wrong… so right… so confusing.

"I can stop," he whispers against my mouth, his tongue parting my lips, his hand cupping the back of my head and tangling through my hair. He taste like Vodka and cherries and smells like cigarettes and cologne. Delicious and dangerous, for many different reasons.

I wonder if he actually would stop if I told him to. I don't want to find out though. Not right now. So I arch my back, pressing my breast into him, while I delve deeper into the kiss, running my fingers along his scruffy jawline, being gentle where the bruise is.

I'm remembering everything that went on between us... God, do I remember... and it feels so amazingly, blissfully good. Each graze of his lips and brush of his fingers feels like it's erasing every unwanted touch over the last couple of months, as if Luke has erasing super abilities.

His hands find my hips, his fingernails digging into my flesh as he forces me closer while he backs up without breaking the kiss. He's moving us somewhere... to the countertop. He leans me back, the edge digging into my back, before he picks me up and sets me down on it, positioning himself between my legs, our hips grinding together.

"Oh my God...." I let out a porn star moan, but am completely unashamed as I try to rip off his shirt, but it doesn't work like it does in the movies and I end up just stretching it out.

He lets out a soft chuckle at my failed attempt, but the noise gets caught in his throat. "You taste so much better than I remember," he says in a husky voice before sucking my bottom lip into his mouth, causing a slow burn to build inside me that only amplifies when his hands wander up the front of my thighs and underneath my dress.

Needing to touch more of him, I sneak my fingers up the front of his shirt and feel the lean muscles flex beneath my hands. His breath falters as if I'm driving him mad. It's different somehow from the last time we were together, like he's more vulnerable.

"I don't want to let you go," he says between kisses as his fingers graze the edge of my panties, his movements rough and sloppy, built by desperation.

Suddenly, I'm reminded why we haven't touched each other in two months, and what I've been doing with Preston for two months, and why I should pull back. If I was a good person, I would. I'd put my parents above my hormones and just tell Luke what I let Preston do to me, how I let him touch me. I know it would get him to stop, but I guess I'm not a good person. Never really have been. And the adrenaline pulsating through my body, instilled by Luke's touch and kisses, isn't helping either.

Keeping my thoughts to myself, I slant against the mirror behind me, surprising him at first as our lips disconnect.

His eyelids lift open. I know he's worried that I'm stopping this, but I grab the front of his shirt and draw him to me until our lips reunite. Then we kiss each other deeply, our tongues entangled, his fingers slipping into my panties and inside me. I bite down on his lip as his touch brings me pleasure, not pain and shame like I thought it would, like Preston's does.

At one point, Luke leans back slightly, watching me as I get lost, drifting away from the reality that I wake up hating every day. Moments later, I fall apart in his arms, gripping his shoulders, holding onto him.

There's a pause as the haze and heat leave my body and mind. I can tell he thinks I'm going to bail—I can see it in his eyes. I have no intentions on doing so, so I slant forward to kiss him again. But right as our lips brush, we're interrupted by a knock on the door.

"Luke, get the fuck out here." Another loud bang and the whole door rattles. "We have a huge fucking problem we need to discuss."

I feel Luke's muscles go rigid as he moves away and stares at the door, trying to figure something out as he scratches his head. Recollection slowly clicks across his face and he staggers away from the door, patting the back pockets of his jeans before rummaging around in all of them. "Fuck, I'm screwed." He pats his plaid shirt pocket and lets out a frustrated breath.

I hop off the counter and readjust my dress over my legs. "What's wrong?"

He swiftly shakes his head. "It's nothing." Without looking at me, he blows out a breath. "You need to go." His gaze finally resides on me and through the drunken dazedness I detect a hint of fear. "Walk out of here, leave this fucking house, and don't come back."

Someone knocks against the door again. "Luke, if you don't get out here now, I'm going to have to bust the fucking door down and that's just going to piss Geraldson off more."

I shake my head, tucking wild strands of hair behind my ears. "I'm not leaving until you tell me what you did," I tell Luke, but then seconds later, I put two and two together "Did you cheat?"

He puts his finger to his lips, urging me to be quiet. "I always do," he whispers.

"We found the fucking ace that fell out of your pocket!" The guy shouts from the other side. There's a deafening bang as he probably rams himself into the door. "I warned you not to do this, man!"

"Shit, we have to get you out of here…" He scans the bathroom for another way out besides the door and into the wrath of a very angry, very big guy who probably has a gun.

It seems like I should be more worried than I am, but this is nothing new to me. I've been chased down by people I've ripped off before, on more than one occasion—it's how I met Luke. I know there's more danger considering who the people are, but at the same time, that sick addiction of mine is manifesting and telling me to bask in it because it'll erase the emotions trying to shove up inside me, emotions Luke's fingers and lips just brought out in me.

Still, I search for another way out of the bathroom and then remember that there's a window near the shower. "Jackpot," I say as I walk over to the shower, step inside, and lift the window up. A gentle breeze blows in as I stare down the three-story drop. Not too bad. Doable maybe.

"Are you fucking crazy?" Luke gapes at me as I pop out the screen, letting it fall to the ground below then stick my head out to calculate what I'm up against. No fences. There are cars down there, but hey, it wouldn't be the first time I had to land on a car before. "We're on the third floor for God's sakes."

"Yeah, but that… could be… doable…" I glance over my shoulder at him and am alarmed by the fear in his eyes. But then I think of his sister and how she committed suicide in an act similar to this and feel sort of bad. Still, the other alternative isn't that great. "I'll go first if you want me to."

Shaking his head, he snatches ahold of my wrist. "I don't want you going anywhere outside the window. I fucking mean it, Violet."

Sighing, I stick my head out, ignoring how tight his grip gets on my arm as I look for other options. Moments later, find one. "There's a fire escape just at the corner… and the ledge is pretty thick. We can walk on it and then climb down the fire escape."

"No." His voice is firm and so is his hold. "I won't—"

He's cut off by the sound of the door being crashed into again, this time to the point where the hinges start to give in. While he's distracted, I slip my arm out of his hand, and hurrying to climb out. *Whoa, head rush.* I brace my hands and back against the wall as the wind slams against my cheeks and hair.

Luke curses under his breath, reaching for my ankle as I balance up on the ledge. My heart thrashes, excited, nervous, terrified. This is everything I need at the moment and I calmly crouch down and extend my hand to Luke.

"Come on," I say calmly. It's terrifying how terror can settle me. "It's not so bad. I promise."

He starts to protest, but the banging grows louder and without any more hesitation, he's grabbing my hand and ducking out, his body shivering, either from the fear of heights or the fact that there's a guy with a gun about to break down the door.

Luke works to catch his breath as he stands beside me, staring down at the three-story fall, his eyes wide. "Shit, this is intense… I seriously hate heights."

Still holding onto his hand, I inch my way across the ledge with my back pressed against the side of the building, guiding him with me. "You act like you've never had to escape out a window before." I cast an amused glance in his direction, feeling way too at peace with the situation, but I can't help it. This is what calms me, what distracts me, what makes the pain of being near him quiet.

He has a tight grip on my hand as he moves with me, continuously keeping an eye on the ground below as his palms become sweaty. "You seem way too calm about this," he notes, his gaze flicking to me. "If I didn't know any better, I'd guess you were enjoying it."

I shrug, not able to deny it. "I think you know me enough to know I'm not afraid of heights."

He pauses, searching my eyes. I feel like I'm a freak on display because I swear to God he sees my dirty, little secret hidden inside me. "No, it's not the lack of fear... but the presence of excitement that seems a little off for the situation."

I try to think of something to say, but come up blank. Gratefully, we reach the fire escape and I put all my attention onto getting down it. I release his hand and duck beneath the bar then jump down onto the grated stairway. Right as Luke joins me, a large guy sticks his head out the window, looking as angry as one of my more abusive foster fathers I had for a brief two weeks when I was twelve.

"Goddammit, Luke!" He rams his fist against the windowsill, debating whether to climb out and chase us or attempt to intercept us at the bottom.

"Go, go, go," Luke urges me with a gentle push as the guy ducks his head back inside.

We race down the stairway, which shakes with our weight. Deep down, I understand just how serious of trouble we're in, but the messed up side of me is thriving, fueled by the danger.

By the time we reach the bottom, I'm nearly dizzy off the adrenaline high. It seems as if Luke can see it on my face because he grabs my arm and helps me keep my balance as we race across the parking lot toward a subdivision near the condo complex.

"Where's your truck?" I ask breathlessly as we round the corner, glancing back at the condos.

Sweat drips down his forehead, even though it's not hot outside. The clouds are rolling in and thunder booms. "I walked here." He pauses near the curb, glancing left and right then behind us. "I need to get you somewhere safe... away from them... and then I'll go... lead them away..."

"I'll go with you." *What the hell am I doing?*

He looks like he has the exact same thought. "You want to go with me?"

I nod, knowing it's so wrong because the main reason I'm agreeing to this is because I want the numbing high inside me to stay. At least that's what I tell myself, not wanting to admit the real reason yet. "Yes."

"I can't... I can't get you mixed up in this... it's not right."

"Too late. I already am. And I did this to myself."

He frowns and I think he's going to argue more, even though he should already know by now that he won't win, but then he gives in and we jog up the street together, heading into the unknown.

Chapter 5

Luke

"I'm in so much damn trouble," I announce the obvious as I shut and lock the door to my apartment behind us. Not knowing where else to go, I'd ran here with a very willing Violet in tow. I have no fucking clue how this happened, not with the Geraldson thing since I'd always known eventually my luck would run out, but with Violet being here. With me. In the place that used to be our home.

Emotions stir inside me as I lean against the door and watch her as she walks around the living room, taking in the food on the counter and coffee table, the textbooks on the floor, the general disorganization of the room that was never here when she was living with us.

"It's messier than when I lived here," she notes, tracing her fingers along a few empty beer bottles on the kitchen countertop and then across a layer of dust on the entertainment center. She pauses, tucking a strand of her red-streaked hair behind her ear, considering something before she turns around and folds her arms across her chest. The excitement that was in her green eyes just a few minutes ago when we were on the ledge has vanished and I'm glad; it was sort of freaking the shit out of me because I think it was stemming from the danger we were in.

"Are you okay?" I ask her, wanting to cross the room and kiss her again, like in the bathroom, but knowing better. What happened back at Geraldson's was us getting caught up in the heat of the moment, being that close together and alone for the first time in months.

She shrugs. "I don't know." She unfolds her arms and thrums her fingers on the sides of her legs as she looks around the living room, everywhere but at me. "What are you going to do?"

I stand up from the door and dare a step or two closer to her, noting she slightly tenses, but thankfully doesn't back away. "I honestly have no idea what I'm going to do. I mean, I've been caught cheating before, but never by guys like that." I blow out a stressed breath as reality crashes on me in a giant, very powerful wave. I've sobered up pretty good since we left the apartment and am seeing a little too clearly for my taste. "I guess I'll just lay low for a while and hope this blows over."

"You really think it will?" she asks, doubtful. "Because I'm not so optimistic."

No, I don't. Not in the least little bit, but she doesn't need to know that. "It's all I can do for now until I come up with another plan." I take another step or two, reducing the space between us, noting how she flinches as I near her, like she's afraid I'm going to touch her again. I want to so fucking badly, but know it's not right and clearly not wanted on her part, so I swing around her and head for the bedroom to pack my bags, understanding that the longer I hang around here, the more likely Geraldson's going to show up.

I expect Violet to leave, but after a minute or two she comes wandering into my room, a room that used to be hers, too. "Where are you going?" She leans against the doorframe, her eyes drifting to Amy's journal sticking out from underneath my pillow. I find myself picking it up and throwing it in the duffel bag.

I shrug, grabbing some shirts and jeans from the dresser and stuffing them into the bag. "I don't know... I'll probably just drive around, stay in hotels for a week or so." I pause, trying to think of where I could hide that doesn't include being with my mother or my father—I swore I'd never ask him for help again after the last time I did and he turned me down.

There's only one family member I actually know, Uncle Cole, my dad's brother who lives in Vegas and who taught my dad how to gamble. I've met him a total of twice. Once when I was five when my dad went there for a little gambling trip and took me with him. And another time when I was eighteen and spent a week down in Vegas while my father was on vacation there, wanting me to come visit. Needing my space, I ended up spending more time with Uncle Cole than him.

I haven't really talked to Cole since then though, except for one or two phone calls, so I'm not sure if my uncle will let me stay there or not. He's not a bad guy, just not the kind of guy you go around asking for favors and help, since he's more like a teenager than an adult. Plus, I don't even have his phone number. There is one way to get it, but I'm not sure if I want to go there yet.

Think of something else.

Violet sits on my bed as I hurry around, collecting my cologne and other stuff, tossing them into the bag, trying to ignore her relentless gaze as it tracks my every movement.

She's here. In my room, like I've been dreaming about for the last two months. But this isn't how I wanted it to go down. Not under these circumstances.

As I'm heading out of the room to the bathroom to get my toothbrush, her phone buzzes from her pocket. By the time I return, she's gone pale, like she's about to throw up. I open my mouth to ask her what's wrong, but she speaks before I get the chance.

"So you're just going for a week, right? To wherever you're going? And then you're going to come back here?"

she asks, fiddling with a leather bracelet on her wrist as she stares at the spot on the floor between our feet.

"I'm not sure..." I zip my bag up and hitch it over my shoulder, rubbing my hand down my face. "This is fucking bad, isn't it? I just need to get the hell out of here. Run away somewhere."

"You can't run away from it forever, Luke." There's an underlying meaning in her tone as her gaze locks with mine and her chest heaves as she struggles to maintain her breathing.

"No, I can't." I pause, dropping my bag onto the floor and retrieving my phone from my pocket to do something I really don't want to do.

I text Toverson, the guy who got me into the game. I need to know how bad it is.

Me: I know I fucked up.

I expect it to take awhile for him to text me back, but it takes seconds.

Toverson: I know. And I fucking warned u. Goddammit, Luke. What the fuck were u thinking?

Me: I wasn't. That was the problem.

Toverson: Where r u now? Ur house?

Me: Can't tell u yet. Not until I know how deep of shit I'm in.

Toverson: Luke, I'm sorry, but I can't get u out of this mess. And warning, Geraldson knows where u live.

A shiver rolls up my spine as I read the text and then moments later, there's a knock on my door, well, more like a pounding of fists.

"Dammit," I curse, stuffing my phone into my back pocket. I start to pace in front of the bed, trying to figure out what the hell to do, but seeing no other alternative. I'm trapped. Violet's trapped with me. This is so bad.

Another loud knock. Then a bang.

"Who is that?" Violet asks, getting to her feet. "Wait. Is it them?"

I stop pacing and look at her. After all this time pining for her to be in my room again, I'm now wishing she wasn't. I messed up big time and now there's going to be some heavy consequences.

"Stay here," I order, then go into the living room to look out the peephole. Sure enough, Geraldson and some big dude with a shaved head that looks at least double my size are standing out there. Both are packing, guns tucked in their belts, brass knuckles on the big guy's hand. My head slumps against the door, a sequences of curses flowing from my lips as I ram my fist into the wall until the sheetrock cracks.

"What are we going to do?" Violet comes up behind me. "And quit beating up the wall. It didn't do anything to you."

I elevate my head and turn to face her. "*We* aren't going to do anything." I stride across the room and shove her toward the bedroom. "*You* are going to stay back in here and hide while I talk to them."

Violet plants her feet firmly to the floor and presses her hands against my chest, refusing to move. "First of all, I really doubt they're here to talk. And second of all, I don't need you to protect me from this. Trust me; I've had my fair share of crazy shit."

"I know you have." I give her a gentle shove toward the bedroom as I hear someone messing around with the doorknob—I'm betting they're trying to pick the lock. "But it doesn't mean that my fuck ups have to add to that list." I start to push her toward the bedroom again when the front door flies open, the doorknob slamming into the wall behind it and leaving a hole.

"Fuck." I strategically place myself in front of Violet, pissed at myself for making bad choices and getting her involved. I don't give a rat's ass about myself, but her...

well, it's making me literally sick just thinking about them even so much as touching her.

"Luke Price," Geraldson says darkly, taking in my small apartment as he enters. The large guy strolls in right behind him, shutting the door and closing us in. "You owe me some money."

Gritting my teeth, I reach into my pocket and take out the fifteen hundred I won today. "There ya go." I throw the small pile of cash on the floor between us, knowing there's going to be more to it than that.

Geraldson bends down and picks it up, fanning through the bills. "You think this is going to be enough?"

"Probably not," I say dryly. "But it's what I won."

He lets out a low laugh, handing the cash to the big guy who stuffs it into his back pocket. "You steal from *me*," he slams his finger against his chest, "and you think we're even because you gave me the winnings back." He cracks his knuckles. "Who the fuck do you think you're dealing with?"

A thousand comebacks tickle at my tongue, but I bite them back, knowing it'll make things worse. If I was alone, though, it'd be a whole other story. "How much?"

He smirks. "Nine thousand."

"I don't have that kind of money," I snap. "And that's six times as much as I won today."

"That's the price you pay for being a fucking cheat," he bites back, stepping to the side to let the big guy step forward. My muscles ravel in knots because I know what's coming. "You were warned not to fuck with me," Geraldson says as the big guy pops his neck and then stretches out his fingers with the brass knuckles on them.

I could run, but they'd only chase me. And throwing a punch means getting more in return. And knowing Violet, she'll probably try to intervene, like she did that time at the bar when I got myself into a mess. I don't want her getting involved more than she is, so I tighten my muscles and hold still as the big guy rams his fist right into my side. The impact of the metal knocks the wind out of me as my body fights to hunch forward, but I refuse to let it, forcing myself to stand tall. From behind me, I hear Violet suck in a breath, then her hand touches my back, causing my muscles to twitch.

"You have five days to get the money to me," Geraldson tells me as he and the large guy head for the front door. "And if you don't, you won't be walking away from this." His threatening tone makes me want to clock him in the face.

Fighting, it's what I do. It's engrained in every part of me, helps me settle down, calms me when there's a storm inside me. But I can't bring myself to do it—not with her just inches away from me.

"And you." Geraldson leans to the side and looks around me to Violet. I have to stab my fingernails into my palms just to keep my hands in place. "You can tell Preston that I won't be doing business with him."

Violet doesn't say anything, just flips him the middle finger as he strolls out of the apartment with the big guy.

When they're gone and the door is shut, I turn to Violet. Her eyes are frantically scanning over my body. "Are you okay? He hit you pretty hard." She starts to lift her hand as if she's going to touch me, but then pulls back, deciding against it.

I nod, allowing my shoulders to slump as I sink down onto the closest sofa. "Super," I say through clenched teeth as I cradle my throbbing side.

"What an asshole; sucker punching you like that." She kneels down in front of me, sweeping her hair to the side as she lowers her head to inspect the area I'm cradling. "Did he break any ribs?"

I fight the compulsion to shut my eyes and breathe in her scent, instead waving her off. "I'm good. Just a little bruise." I give her a stiff smile. "Nothing I can't handle."

"Do you want me to get you some ice?" she asks, leaning back and sitting on her heals. "Or some painkillers?"

"I have painkillers in my room and I'll get them." I get to my feet, moving slowly through the pain. "And no time for ice. I need to get going." Now more than before, to a place I don't want to go, but I know that if I don't pay up, I'm going to be fuuuuucked. And it serves me right. I went there looking for trouble. I got exactly what I wanted.

"Where are you going?" Violet asks, following me as I hobble back to my room.

I want to ask her why she's still here with me. Why she's not running away again like she has been, but I fear asking her will remind her. "I'm going to go gamble and see if I can get up to nine grand."

Her eyes widen as a breath eases out of her lips. "How the hell are you planning on doing that? I mean, you could end up losing all of your money in the process and be even more screwed."

I pause in the doorway of my room, knowing my only option at the moment that might help me dig my way out of this mess. "I have to make a phone call," I tell Violet, my voice sounding strained. I shake it off and grab my phone from my back pocket. "Can you give me a minute?" I ask and then head back to the kitchen to make a call I don't want to make.

As I stand there, trying to dial my father's number, it proves harder than I thought. Still, it's either ask him or get my ass beat to death. Shoving all my pride aside, I just do it.

He answers after a couple of rings. "Luke, I'm so glad you called," he says before I can even utter a hello, sounding so relieved I'm talking to him again. "It's been too long, but I was waiting for you to call like you said the last time we talked… I didn't want to be too pushy anymore."

"I didn't call to talk," I tell him, closing my eyes and pressing my fingers to the brim of my nose, feeling a headache coming on strong. "I… need a favor."

"Oh." The disappointment in his voice makes me feel bad, but at the same time, causes rage to flare inside me for feeling guilty. "What did you need?"

I open my eyes and plop down on one of the barstools at the counter. "I need Uncle Cole's number. I used to have his number, but it got erased from my phone a while ago."

"Oh. Okay. I can give you it." He pauses. "But can I ask what you need it for?"

"No."

"Luke, I... Do you need some help with something?"

"No." I know I'm being a douche bag, but I can't seem to stop myself. What he took from me when he left me as a child, what he left me with, and what it did to my life—what it all stole from me—still aches like an unhealed wound. I have so much anger inside me, eating me away bit by bit, because I can't seem to let it go and just let the damn wound heal. "I just need his number."

"If you need help, let me help you. I want to make up for stuff, Luke."

"Then give me Cole's phone number. That's what will help me."

He gets quiet again and I think he's going to make this complicated, but then he surprises me and gives me the number, which I hurry and punch in my phone.

"Are you sure you don't need anything else?" he asks when he's finished.

"Nope. Not from you." That remark gnaws at my chest and I open my mouth to mutter an apology, but he speaks first.

"Okay then." Now he sounds like the wounded Bambi. "Well, if you need anything, you can always call me. I'm always here."

"Thanks," I mumble, then press *end*.

Deep down, I know that my life might be easier if I just let go of the stuff between my father and I, but it's difficult, especially when I barely understand it. I mean, I get why he left my mom, because he needed to find himself. Self-discovery. And he's happy now with Trevor, his husband, at least it seems that way. I get the need to be happy, but why did he have to leave Amy and I behind? Couldn't he have done all that with us?

"You okay?" Violet's tone carries caution.

I nod, turning toward her, forcing myself to shake off what I'm feeling. "Yeah, I'm good... I'm going to try to call my uncle and see if I can go to Vegas and crash with him for a week."

She lingers in the doorway. "You have an uncle that lives in Vegas?"

I nod. "But I barely know him. I'm just hoping he might do me a favor," I say then dial his number.

After I call him up and have a five-minute conversation with him that mainly centers on gambling, he tells me, "Sure, come the fuck down here. We can totally hit up a few underground games and see what we can come up with." He says it like he understands, which he probably does, since he's a lot like me, just fifteen years older.

I get up to go finish packing, while Violet stands in the doorway, not uttering a word, but the worry in her eyes says a lot.

"What about school?" she finally asks as she shifts her weight.

My obsessive need tries to take me over, but I tell it to shut the fuck up. "I can miss a week. It's not a big deal." I add my container that carries the medicines for my diabetes into my bag.

"You always made it seem like a big deal," she says, plopping down on the mattress beside my bag. "And trust me, if anyone gets that, I do."

"I know you do," I tell her, both loving and hating that we have so much in common; love because of how much I want to be with her and hate because of how much I want to be with her.

"Vegas is really far," she says. "Can't you do the gambling here?"

"No." I keep my head tipped down, knowing if I look up and see her on the bed I'm going to lose it. I need to focus right now. "I just need to get out and get some money made where no one knows my reputation. And I don't want to be hanging out here with Seth and Greyson while I'm cleaning up this mess. This is my mess, not theirs." I pick up my bag from the floor and swing it over my shoulder. "And it's the only option I have at the moment."

She bites at her fingernail, clearly nervous. "For how long?"

I shrug, getting a couple of painkillers from the dresser and swallowing them down with my saliva. If they don't kick in soon, I'm going to be in some serious pain. "For as long as it takes."

"But isn't that a little risky? I mean, you could lose your money and do you really want to be messing around with stuff like that in Vegas. Aren't things like, really intense down there?"

"Everywhere's intense when you really think about it. And it's the only option I have at the moment. And besides, my uncle knows what he's doing."

She's quiet as I go over to my closet to grab my jacket. I hear her phone go off in her pocket again and when I turn around, she's chewing on her bottom lip with uncertainty written all over her face as she reads the message.

Shaking her head, she stuffs the phone into her pocket. "Want some company? I mean, on the road or whatever." She gives a nonchalant shrug, indifferent on the outside, but I can tell she's hiding something on the inside.

"You want to come on the road with me? Seriously?" Something really bad must be going on if she's *choosing* to be around me.

There's so much fear and pain in her eyes that I want to grab her, hug her, and never let her go. The look is a total change from when she was on the ledge of the building and she looked high. I thought she was for a moment, but I think it might have been some sort of weird adrenaline rush.

"I could use the break." She shrugs.

I wonder who texted her a few minutes ago and if it has anything to do with her sudden okayness to be near me. I'm guessing it was Preston and he's angry that she just lost one of his clients. Fucking prick. He probably threatened her.

"I thought you hated missing class?" Excluding the riskiness of her going, I'm still reluctant. It's like I can't get past the fact that it doesn't really seem like she necessarily wants to go with me, so much as she wants to escape something. And the idea of being on the road with her, sleeping under the same roof, when she really doesn't want to be with me, doesn't seem like something I can handle without losing it. And I can't lose it right now. I need to pull my act together and get some cash made quickly.

She presses her lips together and abruptly gets up. "Yeah, you're right. I don't even know why I'm asking." She hurries for the door, but I catch her arm and stop her.

"I'm just wondering why you want to go with me after," I motion between the two of us, trying to find the right words, "everything that's happened over the last couple of months."

"I need an escape, too. I can't... I don't..." She huffs in frustration, finally making eye contact with me. It's overwhelming to the point that my legs almost buckle. "Look, if you don't want me to go with you, then you don't have to let me."

I want to ask her what she needs to escape from, but she's closed off. I know her well enough that she's not going to tell me, not now anyway.

"I want you to go," I say, my grip loosening on her arm. "But I also don't want you to get even further into this mess."

"This mess is a lot better than my alternative," she mutters under her breath. "Trust me."

"Violet, I..." I trail off, realizing that I can press her all I want, but she's not going to open up to me like she used to. I can almost see the wall around her, the one she had before we were together. Only it's twenty times thicker and sturdier this time. "Come with me… I want you to."

"Okay, if that's what you want," she says nonchalantly, but a glimmer of that *I-won* attitude flashes through it, giving me a brief glimpse of the Violet that made me want to change everything about myself—try to be a better person.

"Okay then," I say and it feels like we've made some sort of silent agreement in our exchange, but I haven't read the fine print yet. "Are you ready to go? No, you'll probably need to stop by… your place, right? I mean, for clothes and stuff." I'm rambling, nervous, like a fucking pussy who's never spent time with a woman before.

"I guess so," she says flatly. "I mean, yeah. I need to go… to the house to get my stuff."

I frown, feeling rage inside my chest hotter than a goddamn wildfire as I pick up on a vibe she's trying to keep hidden. "Is there something going on with that fucking douche bag...? He hasn't… he hasn't hit you or anything? Because I'll beat the shit out of him if he has."

"No we're fine—everything's fine." She slips her arm from my hand. "Let's go if we're going to do this. I'll call Greyson on the way and see if he can cover my shifts at the diner." She cringes as if the idea makes her uncomfortable.

I sigh and follow after her as she walks out of my bedroom, knowing I'm making a huge mess and should try to be fixing it. I just can't find the will to stop it so I walk straight into the train wreck.

Violet

I'm in deep shit. I knew this even before I got the text from Preston. The text just confirmed it.

Preston: Just got a text from Roy. Dammit, Violet, you're going to fucking pay for making me lose a client like this. And it's going to be worse than the last time. I swear to fucking God, you're going to owe me for the rest of your life.

The text replays in my head over and over again as I try to get the courage to get out of the truck and go into the trailer house to get my stuff. I don't want to be a coward, but I can't stop thinking about how I've been "paying" for my fuck ups for the last two months, the bruises on my legs marking my payment and my penitence.

It's sundown, the stars are out, and the porch light of the trailer house is on. There's a party going on; cars lining the driveway, people standing out on the deck and loitering in the yard. It'll make it easier to slip in unnoticed, but worse if Preston runs into me. He'll probably be high on something and less controllable.

"I'm going to go in with you," Luke tells me, shutting off the engine and unbuckling his seatbelt.

I want to argue with him because I don't want to rely on him like that, but dammit, I need someone right now. I nod my head and then get out of the truck. When we meet at the front, I don't move away from him, letting his nearness calm me down. I'm not stupid. I know this is all going to come crashing down on me soon, especially when we're on the road and all the unspoken stuff between us comes pouring out. But right now, I just want to pretend he makes me feel safe again, that I didn't run away, didn't mess everything up—that his mother didn't help kill my parents.

When I reach the top of the stairs, I squeeze between the drunk and stoned people blocking our path, and come to a halt in front of the screen door. Preston is in the living room, talking animatedly to his pothead friends with a joint in his hand. There's music playing from the stereo and empty liquor bottles all over the kitchen countertops.

"Maybe I should go in by myself," I say to Luke, but they're just words that have no true meaning behind them.

He doesn't say anything, taking my hand in his. He opens the screen door and we walk into the house. Preston doesn't look in our direction at first, engulfed in a conversation, but when I steer Luke through the crowd to the hallway, he notices. He gives me a dark look mixed with lust that makes vomit burn at the back of my throat. Then he notices Luke and the lust turns to anger.

"What the fuck's going on?" he asks. Abruptly, the entire room is looking at us. Smoke encircles around me, a potent snake that stings at my nostrils and smells like weed and cigarettes.

I'm not one to shy away, but I'm more tense than usual, a reaction linked to the reason why there are bruises covering my leg. "I came to get my stuff." Surprisingly, my voice sounds strong.

Preston lets out a laugh, handing the joint to a tall, lanky guy beside him before crossing the room toward me, shoving people out of his way who look about as dazed and confused as they can get. "What? You're moving out again?" His cold glare lands on Luke. "With this asshole?" Preston doesn't like Luke, considering Luke kicked his ass once.

"I don't know if I'm moving out yet," I say as Luke's fingers wander up my wrist, gently stroking my skin, sending a calmness through my body I've never felt before. "But I need a break from you and all this crap." I raise my chin, voice strong, despite my inner jitteriness.

103

I've always been good at faking it when needed. I can be calm in the snap of a finger even when I'm not. Pretend I don't care when I really do. Act like I don't feel a god-damn thing for someone when really, I feel *everything* for them.

Preston's right in front of me now. I can see that look in his eyes again, the one that came before the bruises that are on my legs. "You're making a big mistake." His voice is low and carries a warning, just like it always does when he's threatening me.

I should have fought more.

Should have bruised the shit out of him.

Should have. Could have. Would have.

"I just need a break," I repeat. *Stay firm.*

"A break from what? Having a roof over your head? Food on your plate? A ride?" He pauses, his gaze flicking in Luke's direction then he leans down in my face, so close I can feel his hot breath on my cheek. "Or being the little whore that you are ever single day. You fucking cunt, you use me to live here—use your little fucking mouth and body to get what you want."

Luke's hand is suddenly leaving my arm as he roughly shoves Preston back, causing him to stumble over his feet and almost fall. "Back the fuck off," he warns. "Or I'm going to make you."

I can take care of this. I don't need you, I want to say, but I can barely breathe, let alone speak. Everyone is looking at me in the midst of my weakness, about to have a meltdown. *I need something. I need something...*

"Bend over," Preston said, pushing me toward the bed. "Come on, V; bend over and take it like you want to."

"What I want to do is knee you in the balls, Preston," I said back. "And if you touch me again, I just might—"

He grabbed a handful of my hair and pulled hard. "And what?" Another tug, but I refuse to wince. Show pain. I am the fucking calm before the storm. I am untouchable. No one can hurt me. "Come on, tough girl; let me hear all the terrible things you're going to do to me."

I wanted to tell him everything, how much of an ass he was being, to get his hands off me, to go fuck himself, but then I remembered how the last time I did, he made me move out and how this time, I wouldn't have Luke to save my sorry ass. So instead, I forced myself to relax as he shoved me down on my knees, which ended up slamming into the side of the bed. Then he walked around in front of me, shoving me back a little and unzipped his pants...

105

"I'm l-leaving for a week or so," I stammer then dodge around Preston, loathing how unsteady I feel, wobbly, like I'm walking a tightrope, about to fall blindly into the unknown.

"You leave and I'm not taking you back this time!" he calls out after me, anger burning in his tone and slamming into my back. "You need me, Violet Hayes! I'm all you got!"

"Fuck you!" I snap venomously, turning and flipping him the bird. "I hate it here and I fucking hate you." *Shit. Oh God. Oh shit. No.*

"You ungrateful little bitch," he seethes, storming after me, his veins bulging, more angry than I've ever seen him, which makes me wonder how hard he's going to hit me if he gets close enough; but I never get to find out because Luke shoves him back again and Preston slams into the wall, stunned.

"Leave her the fuck alone," Luke warns as he follows me through the crowd with his fists raised. "She's way better off not being here. She deserves better. And you're going to let her go or else I'm going to have to make you let her go, you sick son of a bitch."

106

Preston gives a sharp laugh and there's something al-most psychopathic about it, so uncontrolled, so irrational. I know what's coming before he even says it.

"You think she's better than me." He laughs again, his voice following me as I rush toward the hall. "You want to know why I call her a whore? Ask her how she pays her debt to me. She can try to tell you that she doesn't like it, but by the moaning, I can tell that she does."

I cover my ears and run back to the room, not wanting to see or hear Luke's reaction to what Preston tells him next, not wanting to feel the shame on the inside. When I get to the room, I head for the closet to get my bag, but then realize that Luke may not want me to come with him, now that Preston's let that cat out of the bag.

"Fucking douche," I curse under my breath as I stand in the darkness of the room, unsure what to do. I want to grab a razor and slit my wrists, but am I ready to go that far?

Finally, I sit down on the floor, bring my legs to my chest, and rest my head on my knees. "Why, why, why can't I ever stand up to him? I'm a badass to everyone else, but to him, I'm so weak."

"It's not your fault." The sound of Luke's voice makes me stiffen. Great, he heard me in a weak moment. *So weak.*

"He abuses his power as a parent and makes you feel helpless." I smash my lips together and lift my head to look up at him. He's just a shadow in the darkness, unreadable.

I shove my emotions down, wanting to be unreadable, too. "Are you speaking from experience?"

"Yes," he says simply, inching across the room toward me. "My mother abused her power a lot."

It's something that's haunted me since the day I walked out of the apartment—walked away from him. Luke hated his mom, something I learned early on when I first met him. He'd told me a few vague stories about how she's made him shoot her up with heroin. I'm sure that was barely getting to the surface of the problems that woman caused. Part of me had felt bad for blaming him for something she did. It wasn't Luke's fault my parents are dead, but he painfully reminded me of what happened—still does.

"Maybe I shouldn't go with you," I say heavy-heartedly. "It probably wasn't such a good idea in the first place. You and..." I shake the thought out of my head because I want it too much. It's better if I don't go, although, I don't really have anywhere to live anymore unless I'm willing to sacrifice my dignity and more.

He pauses then he backs up to the light switch and flips it on. I blink against the brightness of the light as he searches my face for something—I have no idea what—then he says, "No, you're coming with me. There's no way I'm going to leave you here," he glances over his shoulder at the door, "with him. It's not healthy the way he treats you and looks at you." His gaze collides with mine and a flicker of safeness rises inside me, but it only makes me ache more. "You need to stay away from him, Violet. You deserve better than that." His lips drop to my mouth, but it happens so quickly my brain can barely register it before he's speaking again. "Much, much better."

I want to argue with him, not just about what he said, but about how bad it is for me to go with him. Luke and I have yet to even begin to confront the major thing that tore us apart two months ago, so taking off without dealing with that seems like such an impulsive, potentially disastrous thing to do. However, I'd rather deal with Luke than deal with Preston anymore. Living with him has been a nightmare and I need to breathe without feeling like my lungs are crushing me, if only for a moment.

I get up and pack my stuff, knowing that I'm only running away from my problems and avoiding the ones in front of me. Eventually, I know it's all going to crash down on me.

It always does.

Chapter 6

Luke

We leave Violet's house with a little more confrontation from Preston, but I can tell the guy is a total pussy,
backing down when I challenge him because he knows I
can beat his ass. He makes me sick by how he treats her,
uses her lack of family as a weapon against her. It's like an
obsession—a sick obsession like my mother has with controlling me.

I try not to think about that as we drive out of town and
onto the highway. It's late, the moon bright in the sky as we
head in the direction of Vegas, which is about a twelve-
hour drive from Laramie. Violet is by my side, sitting quietly. Well, sitting in the same truck as me since she's
managed to put as much distance between us as possible,
leaning up against the passenger door. Space. There seems
like so much of it between us, even though I could reach
over and touch her.

For a while, I think she's fallen asleep, her head resting
against the window, her weight leaning against the door,
chest rising up and down as she breathes softly. I'm reaching for the stereo to turn on some music when she abruptly
sits up, looking very much awake.

"So what exactly did he say to you?" she asks, turning toward me and bringing her leg up onto the seat.

I return my hand to the steering wheel. "I'm not sure what you're talking about." Actually, I am, but I don't want to talk about it… don't even want to think about it.

"Preston." Her voice is flat, emotionless, like when I first met her. It kills me on the inside hearing it again. "In the living room, when I walked away. Did he tell you what I've been doing for the last two months while I was staying with him?" She's trying to remain indifferent, but her voice cracks at the end, revealing how much it hurts her and makes me want to hurt Preston more than anything.

"I don't care what he said," I say, gripping the steering wheel tightly as I attempt to focus on the road instead of the anger burning inside me. "I only care what you say." I pause, waiting for her to tell me. It's not like it was a new revelation. I'd seen them kissing in the parking lot earlier today, but still, it feels like there's so much more to it, or maybe that's just me being stupid and naïve, something I never thought of myself as before. "Do you want to talk about it?"

She shakes her head. "Nope."

God, she's so hard to read when she's this closed off. "Do you want to talk about anything at all?" Like the big

111

old stinking elephant sitting between us, taking up most of the room in the truck. Are we ready to go there yet?

She considers what I said, her eyes wandering upward toward the night sky. "Do you still have that sex tape in here?"

What the hell? "Sex tape...? I've never made a sex tape." That's a lie. I did once when I was eighteen and there was this girl who was really into some kinky shit. But Violet shouldn't know about that, nor do I want her to.

Her gaze lands on me, but it's too dark to see her expression. "You're totally lying to me right now. You've made one." Her tone is light, curious. "You know, I'd like to say that I'm surprised, but I'm not."

I relax a little as her playfulness emerges. "Okay, I'm trying to decide whether I should be offended by that or not. Like you think I'm some kind of man-whore." Which I am—was. Not anymore though.

"You don't need to be offended," she promises with a hint of amusement in her voice. "Besides, I'm sure it was an excellent tape."

God, what I would give to see the expression on her face as she sits back in the seat, tucking her legs under her, her thighs barely covered as her dress rides up, making me want to slide over and finish what we started back in Geraldson's bathroom.

Now is not the time to get a hard-on.

"And besides, I wasn't talking about an actual sex tape," Violet continues. "But that music tape I found in here once that was labeled fuck me or something like that."

Hearing her say fuck me makes my dick go rock hard. But there's no trust between us anymore, no basis for her to want me to touch her, no nothing except my longing to get through her impenetrable wall. Trying is going to get me is a severe case of blue balls.

I try to discreetly adjust myself. "Oh, I think it's still under the seat from…" From when you were with me and we were in this very truck, heading out on our very first date. My chest tightens, air constricting, and all I want to do is drink until I can no longer feel my body.

Violet leans forward, lowering her head toward the floor as she reaches under the seat. She rummages around until she finds the tape. "Yep, right where you threw it." She sits up and reads the label. "My Fuck Tape." She turns it over in her hand, a smile tugging at her lips. "It's funny you actually have tapes. Hardly anyone knows what they are anymore."

"The truck came with a tape player and I'm too cheap to put a new stereo in," I explain. "Maybe one day, though, I'll change it out."

She shakes her head as she feeds the tape into the deck. "Don't. It gives the truck character." She presses play then sits back, waiting for a song to come on. For the life of me, I can't remember what the hell's on there.

Seconds later, I cringe as the first song thumps through the speakers. Violet instantly suppresses her laughter as she covers her mouth with her hand. She stays that way, listening to the lyrics until finally she lowers her hand. "So... is that what you call your special man part?" she asks, choking back her laughter as she slaps her hand over her mouth again.

I shake my head at her and playfully reach over and give her a little shove, knowing I'm being flirty right now, but hey, she started it. "Even if I did have a name for my cock, trust me, it'd be a lot better than that."

She continues laughing, her hand over her mouth, her shoulders shaking as she uses her free arm to shove me back. "I can't believe you've had sex to this song."

"Hey, I never said I had sex with anyone to this," I protest, even though I have no clue if that's true. I'm trying not to grin because I never thought this would be happening again, things being so light between us. I don't want to get all excited when I know it's going to crash down at any moment. "And they're not all bad. Some are actually pretty good." I reach forward and fast forward to the next song. Nine Inch Nails' "Closer" comes on and I let it play, relaxing.

She lowers her hand to her lap and absorbs the lyrics silently. I'm guessing if she wasn't so good at shielding her emotions, she'd probably be blushing, but it's not her style. I remember when she told me she was a virgin, back before I took her virginity. She said it so bluntly, so unashamed, that I ended up spitting my drink out on the floor in surprise. The only time I've ever seen her show her raw emotions was the one and only time we had sex. It was the first time I didn't try to hold any emotion back, too, which made the moment perfect until a few hours later when everything fell apart.

Another time, another place, where I wish I could have stay. For a moment everything had been perfect, but it was just the calm before the storm.

"Okay, this one's not so bad," Violet remarks as she lets her head fall back against the seat, her lips part. She's so relaxed. "In fact, I could see how having sex to this could be good."

God, what I would give to have sex with her right now. Right here. To this very song.

I could act on it, but I don't, trying to be the decent guy she was turning me into a couple of months ago. The one who took better care of himself, who didn't drink so much, who wasn't so angry.

As I struggle to keep my hormones to myself for the next hour, this weird sexual tension builds between us as she insists on going through the entire tape. Deftones' "Change" Nickelback's "Something in Your Mouth," "Addicted" by Saving Abel. The list of songs goes on and on, getting hotter and sexier with each one. It reminds me more and more of the one and only time Violet and I had sex. God, I want her again. Seriously, whose idea was this? It's getting so hot in the cab of the truck I crack the window, pretending it's because I'm going to smoke, when really it's to cool the hell down, or else I'm going to end up having an orgasm while I'm driving.

I'm saturating my lungs with nicotine when finally Violet slides forward on the seat to turn the music down. "You have a really dirty mind, Luke Price. Seriously. Where did you find all those songs?"

I shrug. "I was bored one day, so I made the tape. Took awhile, but I was pretty proud of it."

Her eyes glide to me and twinkle mischievously in the moonlight shining through the windows. "How many times have you had sex while the tape was playing?"

I squirm uncomfortably in the seat as I ash the cigarette out the window. "I feel a little uncomfortable talking to you about this," I admit.

"Well, it's a lot easier than talking about all the things we aren't talking about, don't you think?" She sighs tiredly as she slumps back in the seat.

"We could talk…" I take a long inhale off my cigarette and gradually let it out, smoke circling my face, "if you want to."

She tenses as she shakes her head and stares out the window to the side of her. "I'm not ready to just yet." she says quietly. "I want to play make believe for just a little bit longer."

God, I've never felt my heart shatter for someone else more than I have at this moment. I want to pull the truck over, wrap my arms around her, and just hold her. But that's not really what she's asking me to do, is it?

So instead, I eject the tape and toss it up onto the dash. "You know I have three more of these in the glove box."

A smile touches her lips as she sits up and gets the tapes out, going back to playing make believe, pretending that everything is okay, when it's not.

Violet

I fall asleep sometime around two o'clock in the morning and crash right into my nightmare. The one where I'm in the basement, hiding, listening to the sounds of what I think are fireworks but turn out to be my parents' deaths. The nightmare has changed over the last two months into something I don't like.

Luke.

He's the one who comes into the basement that night, just a boy my age, but he's not there to hurt anyone. He wants to help me—always wanting to help me.

"Take my hand," he says as he stands in the middle of the basement, looking right at me hiding in the corner, surrounded by boxes and toys. I don't understand how he can see me or how he can tell that I'm afraid, but he can. "Don't worry. I won't hurt you—I'll protect you."

I shake my head, not daring to move. "I can't."

"Yes, you can," he encourages, stepping toward me. "It's going to be okay."

"But I'm too scared," I whisper in horror as sounds fill the house, ones of pain and destruction.

He kneels down in front of me, his hand still extended out. "She scares me, too, but if there's two of us, maybe things won't be so scary."

I hesitate and then finally place my hand in his, crawling out of the corner. There's a moment where I feel safe as he holds onto my hand, but then I hear another bang. I jerk back, my fingers slipping out of his and the safeness slips from my body as he's pulled away from me. Stolen by his mother as she starts to sing that stupid song, the one that ruined my life.

***

My eyelids snap open as I suck in a large breath of air, fighting my lungs to keep breathing, my body to keep thriving, my mind to stay intact as I grasp onto the edge of the seat.

"Violet, breathe," Luke says from beside me. The truck has stopped moving and the sun is up in the bright blue sky, so I can see the worry on his face. He opens his arms to lean in and hug me, but I can't let him right now, not when the feelings from the nightmare still linger under my skin.

119

"I'm okay," I say in a hoarse voice, leaning back against the door and catching my breath. "I was just having a nightmare."

Luke is the one person in the world who knows what my nightmares are about and I can tell it's difficult for him not to say anything about it, but he manages to keep his thoughts to himself and grabs the door handle to get out of the car. "The truck needs gas," he mumbles, trying to shake off my refusal to let him help me. "Why don't you run in and get something to eat?"

I nod and then wait for him to get out before I climb out myself. I still have on my dress and heels on from yesterday, which are getting really uncomfortable, so I grab some fresh clothes from my bag that's in the back of the truck and head inside the gas station's bathroom to change. I put on my *Nirvana* T-shirt and a pair of jeans, then slip on some flip-flops and pull a beanie over my head so I don't have to waste time doing my hair. I don't bother with makeup, but I do put some deodorant on before heading out.

I wander up the aisles, checking my phone messages before deciding to call and ask Greyson if he can fill in for me at work, despite how much I don't want to because it's asking for a favor. However, I don't have another choice right now.

He answers after four rings, obviously just waking up because I can hear the exhaustion in his voice. "What's up?" he says with a yawn.

"I need you to take over my shifts at the diner for the next week," I say, grabbing a bag of Cheetos from the shelf.

"Why? What's up?"

I pick up a bag of M&Ms as well and then head for the soda section. "Nothing really. I just need a week off."

He hesitates then says firmly, "No, I'm not going to."

I'm opening the door to get a Dr. Pepper, but freeze. Greyson's usually not rude like this to me. That's more Seth's thing and even he's toned it down since we first met, so I'm a little thrown off. "Why not?"

"Because you won't tell me the real reason why."

"There's no real reason." I grab two sodas then let the door shut as I head toward the cash register. "I just need a break. I already told you this."

"I can tell when you're lying, Violet," he says and it makes me cringe. I've never been one for letting people get to know me enough to read me, but apparently Greyson can. "Now, if you want to tell me the real reason why, then

121

I'd be more than happy to fill in for you. But if not, then I guess I'll see you tonight at the diner."

"Fine." I grimace. "I can't make it to work because I'm on a little bit of a road trip."

"With who?"

"Someone..."

"Violet."

"Oh my fucking hell." I drop the food and sodas on the countertop, ignoring the dirty look the fifty-year-old cashier lady gives me for my language. "I'm on the road with Luke okay... heading to Vegas."

"*What?*" He's shocked and I don't blame him. During one of our little after-work-drinking sessions we've been having, I accidentally let it slip out what happened between Luke and me, well, some of it anyway. I'm usually good at keeping secrets to myself, but apparently having friends meant turning into a babbling girl who can't keep her mouth shut or her problems to herself. "How the hell did that end up happening?"

"A freak accident, caused by destiny once again," I say as I lay a ten-dollar bill down on the counter. "Look, I really don't want to give any more details because they're really not mine to give, but you can call up Luke and see if he feels like telling you what's going on." The cashier lady gives me my change and the bag with my stuff as I put the money into my pocket.

"Fine," Greyson sighs. "I'll fill in for you, but you'll eventually give me the details of how this happened and what happens while you're on the road."

"All right, it's a deal." I push out the door and head for the truck, noting that Luke's not there. He must be inside in the bathroom or something.

"And Violet?"

"Yeah?"

"If you need anything, you can call me whenever, okay?" Greyson says. "In fact, promise me you'll check in."

I have my hand on the door handle of the truck about to climb in when he says it, but I pause. I've never had anyone say that to me. Never had anyone worry about me enough to say it, well, besides Luke. Not since my parents died. It makes me feel uneasy, out of my element, exposed, and I'm on the verge of tearing up like some kind of sap. *God, what is happening to me? I used to be so tough.*

I clear my throat several times before I speak again. "Okay, I will."

Jessica Sorensen

"Good. And be careful... And try to stay out of trouble."

"You sound like a parent." I roll my eyes as I toss the bag of food into the truck and hop inside.

"That's because I worry about you," he says as I shut the door. "And care."

I'm not sure how to respond and start choking up again, so I avoid saying anything. "I'll call you later, okay," I hurriedly say and then hang up, my hands slightly shaking as I put my phone into my pocket.

I roll the window down, letting in some fresh air, and rest my head back, trying to figure out when Greyson and I became friends. I still haven't told him a lot about me, like the stuff that's been going on with Preston, my drug dealing, my adrenaline addiction, but apparently, we've crossed some sort of line where he worries about me and where I agree to try and ease that worry by checking in.

"That's a new one," I mutter.

Moments later, my phone vibrates from my pocket. I think it's probably Greyson again, wanting to know what times and days I work since I forgot to tell him, but when I take the phone out and see the message is from an unknown number, a chill goes up my spine and all the feel-goods I had in me vanish.

Unknown: So I'm guessing by ur silence that u don't want to know who did it.

I want to respond that I already know, but I also don't trust the person on the other line. It has to be another bored reporter, trying to get a story.

Unknown: Tell me, Violet, how disgusting does it make u feel, knowing you've slept with her son.

My heart stops—dies inside my chest. I forget to breathe. They have to be talking about Luke in reference to being Mira's son, but how do they know about him? No one does outside of the police, Greyson and me. And the police don't know that I've slept with Mira's son, just that I know him; nor do they fully believe that she's guilty yet, so why would they text me something like this—why would anyone text me like this?

My heart starts thudding inside my chest, blood howling in my ears.

There was someone else there.

There was someone else there.

There was someone else there.

They know.

They know.

They know.

My breath falters as I text back.

Me: Who the fuck are u?

Unknown: u haven't figured that out yet? I guess I'm not surprised, considering who ur parents were. It always took them a while to figure out things too.

I start to shake with rage and chuck the phone without thinking. It ends up going out the window and when it hits the ground, the back pops off and the battery goes flying into a puddle.

"Dammit." I shove the door open and hop out of the truck, picking up my phone and staring at the battery in the puddle. It's useless now. And so is my phone for the moment.

"Is everything okay?" Luke asks as he walks up behind me.

I shake my head. "Not really." Part of me is relieved that they can't get ahold of me anymore, but the other part is frustrated, worried they actually know something and now I've ruined my way of finding out. I need to call Detective Stephner and at least tell him, but his phone number is saved in my contacts.

Sighing, I turn around and face Luke to show him my phone and then point at the battery on the ground behind me. "I think it's broken... I'm going to have to find a way to get a new one as soon as we get to Vegas." I flip the phone over in my hand, trying to figure out if it'll still work with a new battery. There's a scratch or two, but that's it. "Maybe just a new battery though."

"That's fine, but..." he frowns, "what happened? Did you drop it?"

I shake my head. "No, I threw it out the window."

He struggles not to ask why, crossing his arms, an energy drink clutched in his hand. "Can I ask why?"

So polite. "Because I got a text message that made me angry."

He wants to drill me with questions—I can see it on his face—but he doesn't. "Should we hit the road? We still have a couple more hours to go and I'd like to get there before lunch time."

He's changed his T-shirt, but still has the same pair of jeans on. There are bags under his eyes, his lips look chapped, his skin pale, and he's kind of hunching to the left, probably because it hurts where the guy hit him.

"Do you want me to drive?" I offer. "You look tired. And sore."

He shakes his head and raises the energy drink. "No, I'm good. I just need to drink this and… check my blood sugar… I might need a shot… then I'm good to go." Even his voice sounds weary.

I stick out my hand. "Let me drive, so you can get some rest."

He hesitates then stuffs his hand into his pocket and gets out his keys. As he hands them to me, his knuckles graze my palm and I find myself shivering even though I'm not the slightest bit cold. It's obvious to him by the look he gives me, but he doesn't say anything about it as I get in the truck and he grabs something out of his bag.

When he climbs into the truck, he has his small, leather case in hand. He takes out the pen-shaped object that checks his blood sugar and pricks his skin, reminding me of the night when I found him in the bar and had to do it for him. He checks the screen then shakes his head, clearly annoyed as he retrieves another object out of the bag that has a needle at the end. He takes the cap off, lifts his shirt, but then hesitates, glancing over at me with a small amount of wariness in his eyes. I half expect him to tell me to look away. I almost want to, too, but I can't seem to break eye contact, our gazes somehow welded together.

He ends up squeezing his eyes shut like a scared child afraid of needles. His hands quiver as he puts the needle into his abdomen and injects himself. There's something strangely intimate about the moment; I can't even explain it. Like no one has ever seen him do this to himself and he's afraid to let me see it, but also afraid to be alone. I remember how he told me his mother made him inject her with heroin and think that doing this has to be hard for him; painful, aching, and not just physically.

This bubble starts to form around us. Reality slips away. I find myself drifting toward him, wanting to hold his hand, wanting to comfort him, but then, he's done and just like that, the bubble pops and reality comes rushing back to me and weighs me down once again.

Chapter 7

Luke

"The names of the buildings are amusing," Violet remarks, gazing down at a map I had in my bag of the Las Vegas strip. We're parked at a gas station just on the outskirts of the busy city, trying to figure out where to go. It's mid-day, stifling hot, and my truck has no air conditioning so we're practically melting.

"Oh, I want to stay in Caesar's Palace," she says, bouncing up and down in the driver's seat like a little kid in a candy store. She glances up at me and the excitement in her eyes makes me smile just a little, despite how tired I am. "That's the one from the movie *The Hangover*, right?"

I nod, glancing over at the strip in the distance. "But we can't stay there."

She pouts. Actually sticks out her lip and pouts. She's never done that before and honestly, I'm kind of glad because it's like a secret weapon that makes it really hard to say no to her. "How come?"

I slide over in the seat toward her, making sure I don't crowd her space too much. "See all these awesome buildings right here?" I ask, tracing a line up the strip area on the map. "Those are Casino's and you have to be twenty-one to stay in them."

"You have a fake ID though," she says. "Why don't you use that?"

"Too risky," I tell her, breathing in her sweet scent and hoping I'm doing it discreetly. "We have to be careful. And besides, I'd like to save as much money as possible."

She's still pouting as she folds up the map and gives it back to me. "Then where are we going to stay?"

I put the map in the glove box. "With my uncle." I reach for the door handle, internally cringing. I never mentioned to my uncle that Violet was coming with me because I honestly thought there was no way in hell it'd ever happen. So now I'm getting nervous about bringing her with me, not just because my uncle might not be too thrilled, but because of the environment. *What the fuck was I thinking bringing her here? I was thinking selfishly, that's what I was doing.*

"Why do you look nervous?" she wonders as she rolls her window down the rest of the way.

I shrug. "Because of what we're doing... gambling... being here with my dad's brother...." Almost unaware, I stretch my arm across the seat behind her as my chest clenches up. "And because of the environment we're going to be in."

She gives me a look of sympathy, because she knows about the rocky relationship with my dad. She even walked in while I was freaking out during a phone conversation with him.

"And I'm guessing by the wary look on your face that you're going to be playing at places like Geraldson's?" she asks.

"More or less." I dither. "And the place I'm staying at is kind of like Geraldson's, too; at least, it was a couple of years ago."

"That seems kind of dangerous." A strange look crosses her face as if the idea makes her interested in something, as if it being dangerous is almost... turning her on or exciting her. Dammit. It's like we're back on the ledge again and I'm starting to wonder just how much she does this— puts herself in these kinds of situations on purpose. Why have I never noticed it before? Maybe she just didn't do it when we were first together.

"It's not *that* dangerous at his house," I assure her, but it feels like a lie. A gambler, Uncle Cole cheats his way through life. But desperate times call for desperate measures or whatever and he seemed nice enough the last time I visited here.

"Here, let me drive," I tell Violet, giving her a gentle nudge in the side. "It's easier than giving you directions."

We change spots, her climbing over my lap and sending my body into a mad frenzy of need and desire, giving my cock a hard on. But I keep it together and drive down the road, first to the store so she can get a battery for her phone and then we head to my uncle's house that's on the outskirts of town, not so much in the chaos of the city filled with tourists, flashing neon lights, and half-dressed people. The windows of the truck are down, hot air swirling through the cab. Eventually Violet takes her beanie off and fans her face with her hand.

"Holy hell, it's hot here," she remarks, reaching to get her sunglasses out of her purse.

"It gets way worse in the summer," I tell her as I turn off the road onto a side street lined with stucco houses that look the same, yards flourishing with green grass, neighbors outside chatting and smiling. The perfect neighborhood.

"I'm so confused," Violet says as she slips on her sunglasses and takes in the surroundings. "Why are we in the burbs?"

"My uncle lives here," I explain, pulling in front of the two-story house at the end of a cul-de-sac. I put the truck in park and then push the brake on before turning off the engine and putting the keys into my pocket.

"This is so weird," Violet says with a pucker at her brow. "And not what I was expecting."

I open the door to get out. "This is his normal side of life, well, kind of. I'm guessing it won't be that way when we get inside."

Hesitantly, she gets out of the truck and follows me up the driveway, glancing around at the flowerbed beside the pathway, the polished landscaping, all covering up what's behind the front door.

"Welcome home?" She looks even more puzzled as she reads the mat in front of the door. She lifts her sunglasses slightly and gives me a suspicious look. "You know, I'm starting to not buy into this—"

The door swings open and someone lets out a quick chuckle. "Holy shit," Uncle Cole says from in the doorway. He's wearing a t-shirt, black cargo shorts, and no shoes. He looks similar to my dad only he's in his thirties, ten years younger than my dad, and he's rougher with tattoos, gauges in his ears and shaggy hair. "I thought you'd get here a hell of a lot later when you called to say you were on the road."

"We were already halfway here," I explain apologetically. "Sorry I forgot to mention that."

"You don't need to apologize," he says, his gaze flickering in Violet's direction. "I never did like how little we saw of you anyway, thanks to that crazy ass mother of yours keeping you away."

A ripple of anger shoots up my back, not toward him, but toward the mention of my mother. Violet winces, too, so I shove the feeling down and rush to sidetrack the conversation.

"This is Violet by the way," I say, nodding my head at her. "Violet, this is my uncle, Cole."

"Is this your girlfriend?" he questions with an arch of his brows as he slants against the doorframe with his arms folded across his chest. The last time he met me, I'd made it pretty clear how I felt about women and that I'd never actually had one as a girlfriend, only fucked them. So showing up with Violet is confusing him. Plus, he's not the most trusting person to strangers, considering what he does for a living.

"Just a friend," Violet tells him, being very blasé about the whole thing. That stings, even though I already knew it was true. "And his partner in crime."

He seems amused by her, which I don't blame him for—she can be very charming when she wants to be. With a faint smile, Cole stands up straight and sticks out his fist. "Well, it's a pleasure, Violet, aka Luke's partner in crime."

"Likewise." She pounds fists with him and then my uncle steps aside and motions for us to come inside.

It's cooler on the inside—thank God—the fans going, air conditioning blasting and circulating the cigarette smoke lacing the air. The curtains are all drawn shut, so hardly any sunlight can get in. There's some music playing in the kitchen and I can hear some voices, which means he has company, and probably not the family kind.

"I have some people over," Cole tells us as he leads the way through the foyer and into the kitchen, kicking a bag to the side that's blocking the doorway. "And my son's staying with me for a while. You remember Ryler, right?"

I nod, but honestly I don't really remember him that well. I think I met the guy once when I was staying here and all I can recollect is that he's around my age—my uncle knocked up a girl when he was sixteen and pretty much bailed on his family until recently—guess it's a family thing—and that he doesn't speak. The details of why he's mute were never divulged clearly, other than there was some kind of incident when he was about eight.

"He turned into one hell of a card player," my uncle comments, all proud papa, as we step into the small kitchen area filled with smoke from the four guys sitting around the table, puffing on cigarettes. The sound of chips clinking together, the taste of nicotine in the air, the alcohol in the cups, the intensity surrounding the table gets my pulse soaring like a drug addict eyeing crack.

"Ryler," he shouts at one of the guys over the music then walks over to an iPod in a dock and turns it off. "Your cousin, Luke's, here." He points a finger at Violet and me.

A guy around my age glances up from his cards and then takes a sip of his drink. He looks just as intense as when I saw him almost two years ago, wearing jeans with holes in them, eyebrow and lip piercings, a sleeve of skulls and crosses on his arms. His hair is jet black and it looks like he's wearing black eyeliner, but I don't think he is— his eyes just look that way. And he's wearing an I've-been-through-tough-shit expression.

He gives me a chin nod before his gaze drifts to Violet then he turns to his uncle and signs something.

"Is he deaf?" Violet asks in a low voice as she steps up beside me.

I shake my head as Ryler glances over at Violet, clearly hearing her, and my uncle chimes in. "No, he just can't speak," he tells Violet. "But his hearing works just fine."

Violet doesn't ask questions, which isn't surprising, but what she does next shocks the shit out of me. She lifts up her hand and makes these movements with her hand, clearly signing something to Ryler.

This makes him smile, the darkness in his expression briefly lights up as he signs something back, causing Violet to laugh softly then shrug.

"I don't know everything," she says to him. "But some."

I want to ask her how she knows sign language, but Violet has had a very different upbringing from most, living with God knows how many families, so I'm guessing she picked it up somewhere along the way. What I don't like, though, is how Ryler is looking at Violet, like how I used to look at women when they showed up at games— with the intention of getting them on my lap and getting inside them later.

"This is Violet," I say, not even sure if they made introduction already. I casually put my hand on her back, hoping she doesn't shove me away, so uncomfortable in my own skin it's making me fidgety. I want to add, 'my girlfriend,' but that would probably result in me getting kicked in the balls from Violet.

"It's nice to meet you, Ryler," Violet says and I relax at the lack of interest in her tone. She's just being friendly.

Ryler signs something to his dad and my uncle replies, "Actually, we're going to take Luke down to The Warehouse tonight." He goes over to the fridge, gets three beers out, and offers Violet and I one.

I oblige because I'm never one to turn down a drink, but I'm shocked when Violet takes the drink she's offered. She was also drinking at Geraldson's and it has me worried that maybe she's starting to get into the habit, but mentioning it would be like the pot calling the kettle black, so I keep my lips shut, wondering how long the avoidance between us can go on.

Violet

His cousin Ryler was totally eye fucking me in the kitchen, but I have no interest in him. The guy's hot and everything, in a gothic kind of way. Tattoos covering his arms, piercings, black hair that hangs in his eyes and his eyelashes are so thick it almost looks like he's wearing eyeliner. However, the last thing I need is some random hookup where I feel like crap afterward. Not to mention the drama that would come between Luke and me. And I hate soap opera drama.

Then, I found out he's mute and I couldn't help myself. As much as I love keeping my past to myself, I couldn't help but use what little sign language I picked up when I stayed with one of the somewhat normal families who had a son that was deaf. During the four months that I stayed with him, he taught me a little bit when we were hanging out and I still remember pretty much all of it.

After introductions, Luke's uncle takes us up to a guest bedroom, which of course only has one queen size bed because destiny's been on such a roll lately. Cole leaves us to get settled, shutting the door behind him.

As I'm trying to figure out the sleeping arrangement and if I even care, Luke turns to me with his hands stuffed in the pockets of his jeans. "So... where did you learn how to sign?"

I shrug. "One of my foster families had a little boy that was deaf." I drop my bag on the bed. "He taught me a little bit."

"Why did you leave the family?" As soon as he says it, it looks like he bites down on his tongue. "Never mind. You don't have to answer that."

I don't want to either, but I find myself doing so anyway, proving once again how comfortable I am with Luke. "He got sick... the little boy, and with the hospital visits and medical bills, there just wasn't room for a fourteen-year-old girl who had a lot of emotional baggage."

Now he looks like he's really biting down on his tongue, so hard it's probably bleeding. "I'm so sorry, Violet."

I shrug it off, pretending to search my bag for something to avoid looking at him; afraid he might just see how full of shit I am. "It's okay. It was a long time ago... and I've moved on." I hold my breath, feeling him move up behind me, as if he wants to touch me or hug me, but I can't do that with him right now. Fooling around is one thing, but hugging is way too emotionally driven. "So there's only one bed."

"I'll sleep on the floor." Luke puts his bag onto the floor and releases a deafening breath before finishing off his beer and throwing the empty bottle away. "Sorry about this—about everything."

"You don't need to apologize," I say, setting my half drank beer down on the dresser then bending down to unzip my bag and get the battery I bought for my phone out. "I pretty much forced you to let me come with you." I don't bother noting the other sorry he was throwing out there. It feels wrong for him to say sorry for something that was out of his hands. What his mother did wasn't his fault and one day I hope I can fully tell him that.

"There was no forcing. Trust me. I wanted you to come with me more than I should of," he says, sinking down on the bed, his head falling forward into his hands. "Because I'm selfish."

"You're not selfish." I stand back up and open the package the battery came in. I take it out and put it in my phone, crossing my fingers it'll work. "You're anything but."

He elevates his head, his eyes blazing with so much intensity I almost shrink back. "How the hell do you figure that?"

I press down on the *talk* button, shrugging as I wait to see if my phone will boot up. "You gave me my space when I left… when I told you that I didn't want to see you. You gave me what I asked for and that's not selfish."

He gestures at the both of us, gaping. "We're here now."

"I chose to be here." I relax as my phone screen turns on, but any elation plummets when I see that I have five new messages.

Unknown: So we're no longer talking?

Unknown: Did I scare u that bad?

Unknown: Quit being a fucking cunt and text me back.

Greyson: Just checking in on u.

Unknown: U know I should have killed u when I had the chance.

Dizziness overtakes me as I read the last one and have to reach for the bed for support, but end up stumbling and grabbing onto Luke's shoulder instead.

"Baby, what's wrong?" he asks worriedly, his hand grasping onto my hip to hold me upright.

I shake my head, staring over his shoulder at the wall, unable to look him in the eye. "It's nothing." My voice is hoarse as I clutch onto the phone and also his shoulder.

Luke's hand slides up my side, to my neck, and then ultimately cups my chin in his hand and makes me look at him. "What was on your phone?"

"Nothing." I'm struggling to breathe, images of that night flashing through my mind. Is it his mother texting me? Or the other person? The man? The one I never saw?

Luke swallows hard, fighting some kind of inner rage. "Is it Preston? Because I won't let him do anything to you. I promise."

"It's not Preston," I say, finally subsiding down on the bed beside him and frown down at my phone. "You re-member that guy, Stan the reporter?"

He nods, listening intently. "Has he been bothering you again?"

"I don't think it's him," I say, unsure what else to say. I mean, how the hell am I supposed to talk about the killer and my parents' deaths when his mother was part of it? And when she could be the one sending the texts. "Honestly, I don't think it's a reporter at all, with the things that they're saying."

"What kind of things?" His hand finds my thigh, his fingers grazing up and down it, not in a sexual way, but a comforting one.

I close my eyes and give him the phone. "Scroll through the texts from the unknown number." I remain sitting with my eyes shut, listening to his breathing quicken.

"Fuck," he says under his breath and I open my eyes, hovering back at the fury in his brown eyes. His jaw is tight and his hands are now balled into fists, clutching the crap out of my phone. "You have no idea who sent this to you? At all?"

I shake my head. "I've been getting little things off and on from reporters ever since the case was reopened, but this takes things to a whole new level."

"How long has it been going on?" He struggles to keep his voice even and his anger under control. I'm sort of worried that he's going to chuck my phone with how hard he's gripping it.

"They started up yesterday, right before I went to Geraldson's," I tell him. "I need to call Detective Stephner and report it." I pause, reluctant to ask, but needing to do it. "Luke," I swallow hard, "you don't think it could be your... your mother, could it?" Finally, the large elephant that's been hanging out between us has been acknowledged, making the tension between us even worse, if that's possible, especially when Luke remains quiet for what feels like forever. His knuckles turn white from holding my phone so tightly and I swear he's going to grind all his teeth away with how tight his jaw is set.

"I want to say no, but honestly, I have no idea," he finally says through gritted teeth as he gives me back my phone. "She's fucking crazy and I wouldn't put it past her to do something like this." He drags his free hand down his face then leans forward and reaches for his cigarettes in his bag. He pops one out of the pack, puts it in his mouth and lights up, his hand shaking as he flicks the lighter. After a good, long drag, he seems to settle down, but the next words he utters are far from settling. "I'll fucking kill her if she touches you," he says, flexing his fingers as if he's fighting the desire to punch something, like he was doing to the wall back at the apartment.

I don't know what to say. I know it's wrong, the whole eye for an eye thing, but part of me wishes his mother was dead. Just, not by the Luke's hand. There's no way I'd ever want him to carry that kind of burden or suffer the consequences for doing it.

"Hey." I put a hand on his arm, his lean muscles flexing under my touch. "Relax. I'm not even sure if it's her, okay? So let me call Detective Stephner and see what he can do about it."

His gaze fastens on mine. "I'm sorry this had to happen to you." Sincerity pours out of his eyes like hot liquid trying to drown me.

Great, now I want to cry. Jesus, what the hell is with these last few days? I must be getting ready to start my period or something.

Unable to speak, I get to my feet and call Detective Stephner. It sends me to his voicemail so I leave a message telling him to call me as soon as he can; that I've been getting threatening text messages.

When I hang up, Luke's smoking his cigarette and watching me with a look of inquisitiveness. "What can I do?" he asks as I put my phone into my pocket. "Should I take you back home? Please, tell me what can help this."

"Going home isn't going to help." I reach for my beer and take a long swig before speaking again. "If some creep is stalking me, it's better that I'm not there anyway."

"Well, then what do you want to do?" He gets up from the bed and moves toward me, stopping in front of me, holding the cigarette out to the side of him. "You name it and we'll do it."

"We're going to go get you your money," I say persistently with my hands on my hips. "That's what I want to do."

He wavers with uneasiness, scattering ashes all over the carpet, but his uncle doesn't seem like one to care since there was some all over the kitchen floor. "I'd rather you not come with me. It's too sketchy where we're going."

I roll my eyes. "You know what's really sketchy? Going to a crackhouse for your foster mother when you're fourteen because she's as high as a kite and can barely walk, but is sober enough that she threatens to throw you out on the streets if you don't. Personally, I think she just didn't want to risk getting caught," I say. His lips start to part, but before he can speak, I interrupt him. "And I didn't say that for you to feel sorry for me. You just need to understand that I'm not some clueless girl that's oblivious to the dark side of life. I don't need your protection. I've seen it all." I trace my finger up my arm. "And I have skin of steel, baby."

With his gaze locked on mine, he brings his cigarette to his lips, sucks in, then moves it away, smoke snaking from his lips. "I understand that, but it doesn't mean I want to protect you any less." He leans in and brushes his lips against my cheek, smelling of cigarettes, cologne, and beer, all things that are Luke and, for a moment, all I can think is *home*. I want home to be with him again.

The contact of his lips on my cheek causes my skin to scorch and longing to swell inside me. It's so brief, just a flutter of skin to skin, but it's enough for me to remember how mind-numbingly good it felt to be with him.

"I'm going to go talk to my uncle and see what time we're leaving. If you really want to go, then be ready when I get back."

I nod, fighting to keep my balance and keep standing as emotions prickle at my skin. Only when he walks out the door can I breathe freely again.

Chapter 8

Luke

I've never wanted to get into a fight more than I do right now. Someone threatening Violet like that is tearing me to shreds. Worse, there's that stupid nagging voice in the back of my head, telling me it could be my mother. She's crazy enough that if she's somehow found out about Violet, she would do it.

I try to call her a few times as I'm waiting for my uncle to take us to The Warehouse, but of course the crazy woman doesn't answer her phone. Sure, she can call me every fucking hour of the day, but when I actually need to talk to her, she won't answer.

"Give me like a half an hour then we'll head out," Uncle Cole says as I sit at the kitchen table, drinking another beer with Ryler, wishing for something harder, but also wanting a clear head for what I'm about to do. Ryler has a notebook and pen in front of him, our form of communication, just like the last time we met. "You got front money, right?"

I nod, patting my pocket. "Yeah, about three thousand."

Nodding, he starts for the stairway, but then pauses in the doorway. "Luke, does your father know you're here?"

I shake my head. "No. I mean I called him for your number, but didn't tell him why. And I'd appreciate it if you didn't tell him."

"Well, I don't think that'll be a problem since he's pretty much disowned me," Cole says. "Ever since he went on a do-gooder streak a while ago."

"That would make two of us." I raise the beer to my lips and take a large gulp. *Yeah, definitely going to need something harder.*

Cole looks about as uncomfortable as I feel. Usually, I don't say that kind of shit aloud. What the hell is wrong with me? I'm off my game. "Um… yeah… Luke, I'm sorry about that. You know he tried to see you sometimes, right?"

"Yeah, I know," I say, peeling the label off my beer bottle. "Look, just forget I said anything."

He nods, letting it go easily. "I'm going to run up and change before we head out."

Is your girl going? Ryler writes then leans back to throw his empty beer bottle in the trash.

I should correct him that Violet isn't mine, but as far as he's concern she is. "I guess so. I'm not a fan of bringing her, but she's pretty stubborn."

The pen scratches across the paper again. *She looks pretty hardcore. I'm sure she'll be just fine.*

His words gets under my skin, probably because he's noticed her and made assumptions about her solely based on her appearance. Yeah, Violet comes off as tough and she'll tell you the same, but I've seen her break apart in my arms.

I drop it and head upstairs to see if Violet's ready, but when I enter the room, I instantly wish I would have never came up here. Violet is standing there with only a towel wrapped around her, the bathroom door attached to the room wide open, making the air muggy. She has her attention on her bag. Her hair is damp and her skin is dewed with water. My fantasy for the last two months right in front of me.

The sight of her makes me want to rip off the towel and lick every inch of her skin, but I make myself hover back at the door with my fists clenched at my side, mentally telling myself to calm the fuck down. "We're going to take off in like thirty minutes," I say, my voice strained.

She nods, not looking up. "What does one wear to a..." she glances up at me, "I'm assuming illegal poker game?"

I offer her a tight smile. "Whatever you want. You can wear those jeans and that T-shirt you were wearing earlier." *The outfit that covers you up.*

Her nose crinkles as she looks down at her bag. "Nah, it's too hot for that." She bends down and Goddammit that towel rides up her thighs so high that if I was behind her, I know I'd be able to get a view of her perfect ass. "I'm assuming that most of the girls there will be dressed all slutty?" She looks up at me again. "I mean, that is the general theme at these things, right?"

"Yeah, but I'd rather you don't," I tell her, growing the balls to step inside the room and shut the door. She raises her eyebrow with speculation. Sighing, I cross the room and crouch down in front of her, trying to ignore her near nakedness and the scent flowing off her, something fruity that makes me want to taste her. "What are your choices?"

"Well, I have that dress I had on yesterday." She digs around in her bag. "But it smells kind of gross." She pauses, grinning as she grabs a piece of fabric. "Oh wait, I have this." She holds up a short, black dress that's completely see through.

I frown. "You can see through the entire thing." I'm not even sure why I'm being so territorial; it's not in my nature, but the fact that she's not mine and I want her more than I've ever wanted anyone in my entire life makes me want to be sure that no one else can have her. I blame it on my need for control. Violet has never been one to let me control her, which was what partly drew me to her. Although, I'd still like to control her in some ways.

She grabs another article of clothing, an even shorter dress, but it isn't see through. "I'll put this on underneath it."

"I still think you should go with the jeans and T-shirt." I straighten my legs and stand up, telling myself to take a chill pill.

"I'm sure you do," she remarks as she stands up, the towel getting stuck on her thigh so she's even more exposed.

I wait for her to ask me to step out so she can get dressed, but she just stares at me, nibbling on her lip as she holds onto the top of the towel as if she's deliberating something deeply.

"Do you want me to step out?" I should just do it, but I don't want to. I need her to make me.

Her gaze deliberately scrolls up my body. "I don't know."

Be a fucking good guy for once and turn around. "I should probably go."

"Maybe."

"Violet…"

She releases her hold on the towel, an unsteady breath escaping her lips as it falls from her body and onto the floor. "I don't even know what I'm doing," she says, almost horrified. "Just that I want to do it."

I'm fighting to breathe normal at the sight of her; long legs, smooth skin, that fucking sexy as hell tattoo that curves up her side, the way her wet hair drips water down her body, beads rolling down her flesh and across her nipples. I haven't been with anyone in two months and with her in front of me, I lose it. Snap apart. Break. Shattered. So many different things I've never felt before.

Without even processing what I'm doing, I stride toward her, stealing any space left between us. Her lips part as she starts to reach for me, thinking I'm going to kiss her. Instead, I drop down on my knees in front of her and press my lips to her breast, sucking her nipple into my mouth. I don't even know what overcomes me. Foreplay was never my thing. I'm a taker not a giver, but enough people have stolen from Violet that I want to give to her—I'd give everything to her if I could.

I half expect her to pull away; instead, her fingers find my hair and she lets out a moan, causing my cock to instantly get hard. I have to fight the instinct to push her back on the bed and fuck the shit out of her. I nibble and graze my teeth along her skin, making a path to her other breast. I trace slow circles across her nipple with my tongue, glancing up at her face as my fingers wander up the back of her thighs to cup her ass. I'm surprised when I find that she's looking down at me, biting her lip, her eyes glossed over with sheer ecstasy.

"That feels so good," she gasps, her fingers running through my hair, pulling my face closer.

Good God... I'm not even sure what the hell to do with myself. I've never been down on my knees in front of a girl. I've always liked to fuck, but seeing that look on her face, the one I've desperately been missing for the last two months, I want to bring it out more.

My instincts overtake me, ones I didn't think I had. Moving one of my hands to her stomach, I gently push her back until she's leaning against the wall, then I grip her thigh and lift her leg over my shoulder, putting my face between her legs.

I know Violet's not very sexually experienced and it makes me wonder if she's ever done this before. I sure as hell haven't done this—the only oral sex I've done is on the receiving end. The twisted part of me hopes she hasn't because it means just one more experience she's only shared with me.

God, I want her to be mine so badly it's almost torture.

I just wish when it was all over, I could still have her.

Violet

There have been many times where I'm in a moment, wondering how in the hell I got there. Like I can't even backtrack to the second where I made the decision that led me here.

One moment I was standing in the towel, tripping out over life, and how I need to find a way to settle myself down. Since there are a ton of tall buildings in Vegas, I was wondering how hard it would be to get to the top of one of them, but then Luke comes walking into the room and was looking at me with that hunger in his eyes that actually makes me feel want instead of disgust like I do with most guys. I started thinking of how the last guy that touched me was Preston, how he made me get down on my knees, shoving me so hard that I bumped my leg on the side of the bed. Then he grabbed my hair and made me suck his dick. I want to erase the memory, not have it so fresh in my mind, so I dropped the towel, hoping for... well, I wasn't sure, but definitely nothing as amazing as this.

Luke's face is between my thighs, one of my legs hitched over his shoulder, his mouth licking and pulling and sucking and nibbling, making tingles and sweltering heat shoot throughout my body. Never has a guy touched me like this. The guys I've known were always takers. Luke seemed like one of those guys when I first met him, but I learned quickly that his rough exterior was very misleading. He's not the guy everyone thinks he is; at least, not when he's with me.

I let go, relaxing against the wall, as he continues to work wonders on me with his mouth, his fingers digging into my thighs, pressing into my bruises, but I don't feel the pain. All I feel is that wonderful sensation of freedom as heat builds inside of me. I grip onto Luke as I fall into the center of it. I end up pulling on his hair roughly, but I'm too incoherent to release my hold. It doesn't seem to bother him as his tongue and mouth continue to take me all the way to the end, until I'm coming down and breathing profusely. Then he starts to pull back, but pauses, his fingers grazing one of the bruises on my knee.

"What happened here?" he asks, his voice so low and husky it causes vibrations across my skin, almost to the point that I think I'm going to orgasm again.

"I fell," I lie, bringing my leg off his shoulder, feeling bad for not telling the truth, but the truth will only hurt both of us and we've shared enough pain to last a lifetime.

He catches me as I'm starting to walk away and then delicately traces the bruise pattern down my skin. "You know, I can tell when you're lying."

"Please don't ruin this," I say softly. "Please just drop it... I can't tell you... not right now." God, how wrong would that be? Right after he gives me oral sex for the first time, I say *oh, hey, by the way, I gave Preston a blowjob, so recently that I still have the bruises.*

He wants to argue with me to tell him because that's what we do—argue, banter—and most of the time I enjoy it, but he gets up instead. His lips are still wet from me as he leans in to kiss me, giving me the rush I so desperately need from the naughtiness of the whole thing.

His tongue slides deeply into my mouth and our tongues briefly tangle before he pulls away. He tucks a strand of my damp hair behind my ear and looks me directly in the eye, as if he's about to say something important. "If I ever find out that he hurt you, he's going to pay," he says firmly.

I don't have to ask who *he* is. I know who he's talking about just like he probably knows where the bruises came from—well, from Preston; maybe not the blowjob part— even though I didn't tell him. It gives me insight to him. I mean, before I took off, we'd only known each other for like a couple of months and barely were together for a few weeks.

I only saw this protective side of him twice; once with Preston and once with the reporter, Stan. I'm learning, though, that it might be his thing and I both love and hate it. Hate because I don't want to rely on anyone to protect me like that—I'm too strong for that and relying on people will only break me and make me weak when they become unreliable. And love, well, because I've never had anyone do that for me. It's always been me against the world. But part of me wonders, if I could ever, possibly, maybe, let go of the past enough to really be with Luke, if it could be me *and* him against the world.

But that might be me just wanting to stay in the land of make believe.

Chapter 9

Luke

Perfect. Perfect. Perfect. The night started that way, but the moment of elation from being with Violet quickly dissipates the moment we leave that room and I realize I'm not nearly drunk enough for what lies ahead for the night. Before we take off to The Warehouse, Uncle Cole pulls me aside to remind me of the rules, which reminds me of the risks I'm taking. It's kind of stupid when I think about it. I fucked up by cheating while gambling and now I have to cheat again while gambling to make up for it. If I mess up, I'll be right back where I started, only I'll owe two assholes money.

For this very reason, I try to keep Violet out of the loop of what the plans are, but the problem is the girl knows her shit.

It's nearing eight o'clock, but the sky is still bright, the sun blaring it's heat down on the city and desert land that surrounds it. We have the windows rolled down, but it still doesn't help with the sweating factor. Part of that might be because I'm in the backseat with Violet, trying not to be so damn nervous about the entire situation.

"So what's up with this The Warehouse place?" Violet asks from the backseat of Cole's 1970 Dodge Challenger. She's wearing that short dress I didn't want her wearing and it hugs her body perfectly, leaving little to the imagination. "Because it sounds like a place where the mafia would hide dead bodies."

Cole glances at her in the rearview mirror inquisitively while Ryler smiles, rolling his window all the way down.

"Well, if it was, I'd think you'd be a little worried that we're taking you there, wouldn't you?" my uncle jokes as he retrieves a pack of cigarettes from the dash.

"You would think so," Violet says amused, the hot breeze flowing through the cab blows stray strands of her hair into her face. "But if you guys are in the mafia, you're not very scary, nor are you packing a gun, so escape seems possible."

"And how do you know we're not packing any weapons?" Cole asks, his gaze landing on me. I can tell he approves of Violet, which would be just great except that she doesn't approve of me.

"Well, you're both wearing tank tops and there's no place to hide them in there. None of your pant or short pockets look bulky and I made a mental note that neither of

161

you had one in the back of your pants." She relaxes back in the seat, folding her arms, restraining a smile.

"Smart girl," Cole remarks as he slows the car at a stoplight. The busy sidewalks are buzzing with excitement, neon lights flashing on every building, and I can practically smell the slot machines in the inside of them. "Luke, I like this one. You should keep her around."

So do I, I want to tell him, instead I say, "Yeah, she's not so bad, I guess." I nudge her in the side with my elbow so she knows I'm messing around.

"What can I say, I like to prepare myself," Violet says, not moving away when I rest my shoulder against hers. "You never know who the crazies are."

My body stiffens, wondering if she meant it how I took it. But she seems calm and content, so I'm guessing she's just chatting and didn't really think much of it. Still, it reminds me that one of those 'crazies' she's referring to is my mother and what one of those 'crazies' did was murder her parents, which led to her spending most of her childhood in foster homes, which led her to Preston's and her messed up life. All because of my mother and some unknown guy.

Ryler rotates in his seat to look at us and signs something to Violet, something amusing I'm guessing with the way Violet laughs and he smiles.

Violet shrugs. "Knives aren't scary. You can run from knives."

Ryler's brow arches as he rests his arm on the back of the seat, still signing.

"It sounds like I'm speaking from experience, huh?" Violet muses as Ryler nods. Then Violet shrugs again, not willing to divulge any of her past, something I'm used to. I know enough about her, though, and she had a shitty childhood, so I wouldn't be surprised if she ran from someone with a knife. Fuck, what if it was my mother. I never did get the details of what exactly happened that night.

"You're a pretty tough chick," Cole remarks then looks at me. "You know, we could use her tonight."

"No," I say sharply. "She's not here to get involved in this."

"Well she's here," Cole says, getting a little annoyed. "So technically she's already involved."

"She's just here to watch," I argue, balling my hands into fist. "Nothing else."

Violet's eyes are on me, not necessarily glaring, but she doesn't look happy either. "What's up with you and the whole protective thing?" she says it quietly, but Ryler still hears her and sensing a fight, turns back around in his seat and proceeds to smoke.

"I just don't want you getting hurt," I tell her with a shrug. "It's not like this is some new fucking revelation. I was the same way while we were..." I want to say dating, but were we really ever officially dating? Yeah, we went out on one or two dates, but our relationship was so brief—too brief.

"I don't need protection," she promises in a firm tone. "And if there's some way I can help, then I want to. Trust me, manipulation is my gift."

"I don't want to be the Preston in your life," I utter it so quietly it can barely be heard.

She sucks in a slow breath while her hand absentmindedly wanders to the bruises on her legs, pretty much confirming my suspicions that the bastard put them on her. It makes me see red again like when Preston kissed her in the parking lot of the university. My anger blinds me to the point that if Preston was around, I'd do something irrational and probably irreversible and not even think twice.

I remember when Kayden beat the shit out of this guy, Caleb—the same guy who raped my sister right before she committed suicide by jumping off a roof—because he'd hurt his girlfriend, Callie, probably in the same way he hurt my sister. At the time, I sort of understood why he did it, protecting the people you care about. But he'd only been with Callie for a little while so there was still some confusion how he could get so passionate about defending her. I get now, why he did it, how the rage can consume you to the point that you can't see or think clearly if you care about someone that much. I'd have beaten the shit out of Caleb, too, if I ever found him—still would—for Amy. And I'd hurt Preston just as equally if not more for what he's done to Violet because I care about her *that* much, in a way that I'd ruin my own life if it meant she'd have to carry less pain in hers.

I get a revelation at that moment, one that I didn't see coming and I'm not sure if I'm ready to accept it. It crashes into me like a truck, slams the breath out of me, and makes my heart ache in a very unfamiliar way.

I care about Violet more than I care about myself.

Maybe even… love her?

Fuck, am I in love? No, there's no way. I don't even know what love is.

"You're not Preston," Violet interrupts my panicking thoughts, her hand covering the bruise on her leg. "I want to help you if there's a way. You're not forcing me to do anything—I'm choosing to do it."

165

I want to ask her what he forced her to do to cause those bruises, but even if she would break down and tell me, I don't want it to be in the car with Ryler and my uncle pretending like they're not listening while I flip out and probably lose control in the worst kind of way.

"She could be a good distraction, Luke," Cole says as he makes a right off the freeway and up an off ramp. "She's a beautiful girl—and I mean that in a nice, nonflirting way." He's annoying the shit out of me right now and I know he can tell, but doesn't care.

"What exactly are you thinking?" Violet scoots forward and crosses her arms on the back of the seat. Her hair is pulled up so I can see the back of her neck and the dragon, along with the stars tattoos, the ones that represent her parents' deaths.

I don't know why I do it, but I find myself putting my finger to one of them and tracing the pattern. She jumps from the contact, yet doesn't say anything.

"There's this guy, Catterson, who's a total dipshit when it comes to women, but good with cards," Cole explains as he flips on the blinker. "If you sit near him and try to get him to run his bets high, it might help end the game end quicker and give us a better chance at getting out of there with no problems."

"Just how dangerous is this?" she asks warily. "I mean, what problems are you talking about? Like the don't-come-back-here-if-you-get-caught-cheating kind of problems or the you-won't-be-walking-out-of-here-if-you-get-caught-cheating kind of problems?"

"You should probably have Luke answer that," Cole replies, glancing over his shoulder at me.

Violet faces me, chewing on her bottom lip, which is stained with red lipstick, tempting enough to bite. "How bad is this place? Worse or better than Geraldson's?"

I gently cup the back of her neck. "Worse," I say and her body goes rigid.

She quickly shakes off her uneasiness, putting her hands on my shoulders and her mouth beside my ear. "You sure you want to do this?" she whispers in my ear. "I still have some of Preston's weed on me. It's not nine grand worth, but it could be a start."

"No, no drug dealing." My hand finds her waist and my fingers enfold around her as I pull her closer, nearly shutting my eyes at the feel of her warmth. Despite the shit with my mother, I'm still bad for her anyway. Having her here, ready to help with this, is stupid—I'm stupid. "God, I wish we'd been brought together again under different cir-cumstances... I miss you, but know I can't have you..." I don't mean to say the last part aloud, it sort of just slips out and there's no taking it back.

I expect her to jerk away, so it's surprising when she doesn't. She presses a soft kiss to the tip of my earlobe. "I'm going to help," she says then she turns around in the seat, ready to put herself in harm's way, all because of my dumbass. "So what should I know about this Catterson guy?"

Chapter 10

Violet

Let the fucked up adrenaline addiction begin.

I could tell Luke didn't want me to get involved. After being with him like we were up in the room, I'm in desperate need of some unemotional time, the razors and prickles are coming in waves as I struggle to keep my emotions toward Luke obsolete. So I seize the opportunity to distract Catterson, who turns out to be a thirty-something-year-old pervert who likes flannel and smells like pot. Jesus, what is it with me and this type? It's like I draw them to me, like a flame draws a moth.

Still, like I pro, I get a few drinks in him and end up sitting beside him in The Warehouse, which turns out to be exactly what it sounds like—a warehouse full of boxes, but what they're full of, I have no idea. There are five tables that have five players at each, mostly men, although there are a couple of women playing. They have some classic rock playing low, money being thrown away left and right, smoke circling the air, drinks being passed around—a lot of them being consumed by me. I'm not even sure why I'm drinking. I just planned on having one, but then I felt relaxed and one turned into another and another and, well, you get the picture.

"So what do you think, sweetheart?" Catterson places a hand on my bare knee right on top of one of the bruises. I have to fight the compulsion to shove him away and slap his face. "Should I go big or play it safe."

I dazzle him with my aren't-I-so-pretty-and-innocent smile. "What's that saying…? Go big or go home?"

"I like your way of thinking." He winks at me as he puts in his ridiculous bet. I force myself to giggle while I twirl a strand of my hair around my finger. As he waits for the rest to either fold, match or raise, he leans into me and says in a hushed tone, "You are legal, aren't you?"

Fucking dumbass. "Of course," I say with another giggle. "Do I really look that young to you?"

He slants back and lets his pervert eyes lazily scroll over my body, taking an extra long time at where my dress starts to cover my legs. "You look fine as hell." He says it as if it's a compliment, as if hell's a fine place and that being good looking will make me a silly girl who swoons into his arms—who uses the word swoon?

"Thank you," I say like an airhead. Jesus, all I need is some bubblegum and I'm one step away from being a ditz.

He nudges my half full drink in my direction, a vodka and cranberry. "Drink up, beautiful."

I can tell he thinks I'm going to get good and wasted, go home with him, and get freaky. Honestly, I'm getting to the wasted part, so my cattiness is starting to come out, claws and everything. Oh, claws... and Luke's skin... I shake the fogginess in my head. *Focus, Violet. And stop drinking so much!*

Catterson is still grinning at me and I have to force myself to grin back. There's no way I'm going home with this guy. I have my eyes set on the smoking hot guy sitting across the table; intense brown eyes, soft hair, smells like familiarity and everything I wish I could have, but am scared as hell to take because of what it'll mean—facing my emotions head on. Seriously, if there weren't so many damn people around right now, I'd crawl across the table and attack him... rip his clothes off and bite him, lick him, do all kinds of naughty things to him...

That thought has me looking down at my glass, wondering just how much I've drank. It's empty now. Crap, I can't even remember finishing it off... and is it my fifth, sixth... eighth? Dammit, this is bad. Drunken Violet is reckless, wild and impulsive. She can easily get out of control, worse than sober Violet. I should get up and go sleep it off in the car... yeah, I'll do that, just after I do another shot with what's his face.

"Bottoms up," he says as he hands me a shot glass full of black licorice scented booze—probably jager. He lifts his own glass and chugs the whole thing down in one swallow.

I put the rim of the glass to my mouth and knock it back in one gulp, licking my lips and plopping the empty glass down on the table like I'm some kind of badass shot taker; but I'm not and I instantly regret drinking it as my stomach churns. Vomit burns at the back of my throat... I think I'm going to throw up. *No, don't do that. Suck it up.*

"You going to be okay there?" Catterson asks, putting his hand on my shoulder to steady me as I start to tip sideways in the chair.

I make my damn lips turn upward, forcing myself to suck it up—be tough Violet. The one that sells drugs and dazzles costumers. "I'm good," I tell him, managing to smile again, which he gladly reciprocates.

"A little strong for you, huh?" he asks and then doesn't wait for me to answer. "That's okay. We'll get you one of those little fruity drinks," he says and I have to resist the urge to let my smart mouth fly. Grinning, he turns back to his cards, losing the hand and cursing under his breath, but when he looks at me he simply says, "You win some, you lose some."

"I have a feeling you're going to get lucky the next hand." I wink at him and let my fingers drift to the low neckline of my shirt. *God, I'm good*, I think to myself as I see the bulge in his pants

"I sure hope so," he says, adjusting himself as he picks up his newly dealt cards and observes them with a serious look on his face.

I take the opportunity to sneak another glance at Luke sitting across from me. His uncle and cousin are spread out at different tables. In the car they explained that it was pointless to play against each other, especially when they're all cheating. Evidentially, cheating is some kind of family thing or something, at least on his father's side. Although, Ryler didn't seem to into it. In fact, he acted like he was only here for his father.

Luke's been pretty quiet the entire game, sipping on Bacardi and smoking his cigarettes, up quite a bit. I know him well enough to know he's cheating, but I can't tell what hands he's cheating on, which is probably a good thing.

As I continue to openly stare at him, he assesses his cards as the bids make their way around the table. When it's his turn, he puts in about two hundred chips then sits back in the chair, appearing relaxed as the dealer turns over a card. Keeping his cards in one hand, he takes a long sip of his drink, then a deep drag of his cigarette, seemingly oblivious to my excessive gawking of him. Or at least, that's what I think until he glances up at me over his cards, his lips quirking as he winks at me, making me wonder if he was aware of it the entire time. It makes little butterflies dance in my stomach, which has never happened before. Then again, it could be the jager and vodka that's doing it, not butterflies. Oh, who the hell cares what it is. I want him. I don't even care that I'm drunk. I need to do something reckless tonight to still all this energy inside me and right now, I want that something to be him, even though he's the cause of the energy.

Game end soon please. My thighs are burning.

I squeeze my legs shut and attempt to be as patient as I can, watching the players dwindle around the table, while remaining my charming self to Catterson. Finally, the damn thing comes to an end, Luke winning over nine grand, while his uncle and Ryler lose all their money. Well, at least that's how it appears, but I overheard them in the car. Cole and Ryler were to lose to make it not look so suspicious and in return, Luke gives them each a third; so technically, he's only up three grand.

I wonder if he'll be able to make enough and what will happen to him if he doesn't. Being a realist and knowing something about Geraldson's world, I have two pretty good ideas. One, Luke will get the shit beat out of him, pretty badly. I'm not sure if they'd kill him, but just thinking about it makes me sick to my stomach. Or two, Luke will end up not going back to Laramie, deciding it's better to stay away than return to the risk. That option surprisingly makes me sick to my stomach, too.

"So where you heading now, you sexy, beautiful thing?" Catterson asks, the sound of his voice forcing me back to reality. I realize I've lost a little bit of time while I zoned out. Everyone has already started clearing out and Catterson is looking at me expectedly, like I'm about to fuck him right here in the open. "You gotta head back or do you want to come to the back room with me? Because I'd love to see that fine ass of yours in my hands."

There are so many things I want to say to this guy. Like for starters, asking him if that ridiculous line has ever worked. However, I know I have to keep my mouth shut and say the right thing; otherwise, I'll be busted.

I don't know what the back room is, but I have some ideas. Back during my time living on the streets, I ended up sneaking into a strip club with this dude who said we could score some beer from the backroom because it was easily accessible without anyone seeing us. Turned out, the backroom didn't hold beer, but naked women giving out blowjobs and lap dances. Yep, way to awaken me to my sexuality.

She's actually got to hitch a ride with us. Ryler appears by my side and causally puts and arm around me, all knight in shiny armor, signing. *Gotta make sure she gets home safe.*

Catterson glances from Ryler to me and I give him my best I'm-so-sorry-but-not-this-time smile. "What's he saying?" he asks confusedly.

"He says he needs to get me home safe," I tell him, giving him my best I'm-so-sorry-but-we-can't-hook-up look.

"She's family?" he asks Ryler with a doubtful look, like he can't possibly make out the family resemblance.

Cousins, Ryler mouths, giving me this weird side hug thing before he steers me along with him across the room, past the tables, and toward the exit doors, waving at Catterson before opening the door and then we step outside.

"Awe, thanks, cuz," I say with a sarcastic grin as I step out into the dark parking lot and overheated desert air. The street is a little ways away, but pretty vacant, with the city in the distance, a cluster of sparkling lights that dance against the night.

Ryler smiles as he lets the door shut behind him and then his hands move in front of him as he signs, *Hey, it was better than letting you come up with an explanation as to why you flirted the fuck out of him the entire night, but aren't going to let him bang you in the backroom.*

"Hey maybe I wanted him to bang me in the backroom," I state, elevating my eyebrows as I walk backwards, facing him. I'm getting feistier by the second and the need for Luke to get out here soon grows, or I'm going to end up doing something stupid probably.

Ryler pauses in the middle parking lot, confusion masking his face as he messes around with his eyebrow piercing. *Aren't you with Luke, though?*

I stop walking and put my hands on my hips. "Does it look like I'm with Luke?" I'm all talk, though, because all I want to do right now is be with Luke.

I have no idea. He massages the back of his neck easily. He kind of reminds me of Luke in a way, a little squirmy when I'm blunt, but not enough to drop the subject. He's also rough looking like Luke, especially in the eyes, and the piercing and tats add to the intensity. But whether that's for show or not, who knows. *But it looks that way.* He pauses, waiting for my answer. I don't have one to give him because I'm still trying to figure that out for myself.

"Where is Luke?" I scan the parking lot, my eyes landing on the dark purple Dodge Challenger we drove over in, parked toward the back, completely vacant at the moment. The situation could be dangerous, a girl and a very strong looking guy all alone with no one to hear her scream. My sick obsession to walk on the line between life and death pulls me forward, though, instead of back toward the light coming from The Warehouse.

Ryler starts for the car with me, swinging the car keys around on his finger. *He had to go cash out.* He unlocks the door, opens it, then flips the seat forward so I can get into the back. *My dad went with him just to make sure there aren't any problems.*

I point a finger at him as I lower my head to duck into the car. "Again, sounds very mobsterish." I hop into the backseat, very ungracefully and unlady like, probably flashing Luke's cousin my lady part since I forgot to pack underwear so I'm commando right now. I'd care, but I'm too drunk to give a crap and if Ryler saw, he's enough of a gentleman that he doesn't say anything, quietly putting the driver's seat into place before sitting down in it with the door open, his feet planted outside on the ground.

He pops a cigarette into his mouth and lights up, suck-ing in a long inhale as he turns the ignition on. The stereo clicks on and "Red Light Pledge" by Silverstein flows from the speakers.

You seem like a very interesting girl. He grazes his thumb along the end of the cigarette and little pieces of ash dance through the air.

"Interesting?" I rest my arms on the back of the seat as he sits back and leans against the steering wheel to look at me. "That's a nice way of saying I'm a weirdo. But that's okay; I've been called worse."

And better a weirdo than ordinary, right?

"Exactly." I tilt my head to the side and assess him over. He seems like the kind of guy I could potentially hook up with and in the past, with as drunk and bored as I am, I might give it a go. It might be easier than screwing around with Luke, which is going to happen if I have it my way, but even through the vodka and jager, the emotions I've been attempting not to acknowledge the entire night, I can feel this pull toward Luke. And it's terrifying, thinking about what that could possibly mean.

"Mind if I have one?" I nod at the cigarette in his hand.

His eyebrow crooks. *You smoke?* he questions, probably because I've been around smokers the entire night and haven't smoked a single one.

And normally I don't, but tonight I'm going to be someone different. "Yep." Hello world, meet drunken, smoker, Violet.

He shrugs, then takes the pack out of his pocket and gives me a cigarette and his lighter. I light up, not choking on the smoke because I have smoked in the past, under very strange circumstances when someone who took care of me for a while would have me light up for her when she was doing things like cooking and didn't have free hands.

"How well do you know Luke?" I wonder curiously as I take a drag and smoke fills my lungs.

Ryler flicks his cigarette, sending ashes across the gravel just outside. *Not very well. I met him once when he stayed with my dad a couple of summers ago, but that's about it. Honestly, I've barely seen my dad, though, up until a couple of years ago.* He puts the cigarette to his lips and breathes deeply, trying to cover up his uneasiness with the subject. *What about you?* he mouths, smoke laces from his lips.

"How well do I know Luke?" I ask and he nods. I waver, uncertain how to respond because it seems like I know

Luke well, but at the same time, I don't know him at all. "I'm still trying to figure that out," I say truthfully.

What about you?

"What about me, what?" Hasn't he already asked that question? Or am I losing track of time again.

I hardly know you. His attitude is veering toward flirty which would be fine if it wasn't for Luke. Jesus, why can't guys and girls just be friends?

"I'm a fairly boring person," I tell him, then lean forward over the seat with a sarcastic, dark look on my face. "And if I told you anything about me, I'd have to kill you."

He gives me a blank stare, trying not to laugh. *Like I said, interesting.*

I sit back and take a puff off my cigarette. "And I was just going to say the same thing about you, until you started flirting with me."

Hey, you can't blame a guy for trying. He presses his hand to his heart and sits up straight in the seat. *Besides, if you would have just said you were with Luke, then I'd leave you alone.*

Oh, I get it now. He's trying to get me to confess. I'm about to say it to—it's on the tip of my tongue even though I'm not sure if it's the truth—but then Luke and Cole show up and interrupt me before I can. The revelation itself makes panic soar in my chest and the need to do something crazy press up in my lungs and crush the air out of me.

Saved by the questionable boyfriend. Ryler winks at me then gets out of the driver's seat and rounds the front of the car to the passenger side, while Cole flips the seat forward and Luke climbs in the back beside me

As soon as he gets settled, he takes one look at the cigarette in my hand and his brows dip together. "What the hell are you doing?"

I bat my eyelashes innocently at him and extend the cigarette toward him. "I lit it just for you."

He looks at me skeptically. "Yeah, right. And smoked half of it." He reaches for it to test me, but I move my hand to the side.

"No way." I put the end into my mouth and allow the smoke to smother my lungs. "It's mine now. You're going to have to fight me to get it," I say as Cole starts the car and then drives forward out of the parking lot.

Luke flicks a glance to Cole, then Ryler, then shakes his head, restraining a laugh. "How much did you have to drink?" he asks me in a low voice.

I shrug, watching the blur of colors zip by the window as we drive onto the road and toward the freeway that will take us back toward the city. "Five, eight, eleven." I hold up my fingers, trying to show him the amount, but eleven proves to be a problem. "Hey, I was just doing my job. It wasn't my fault that Catterson guy kept offering me drinks."

"You did a fine job," Cole comments, making a turn onto the freeway. "But we're going to have to find a new job for you tomorrow, so the bosses won't catch onto you."

"Okay, at first, I was joking about the mobster thing before, but now I have to wonder." I slant forward to stick my hand out the window and ash the cigarette.

"No mobsters, just hardcore gamblers who don't take shit from anyone," Cole says, putting a cigarette between his lips and cupping his hand around the end of it to light up.

After that remark, Ryler and him start having a conversation about the game, Ryler signing the entire time and seeming really annoyed at his father about something. It leaves me distracted enough to focus all of my attention on Luke as a darkness in my chest starts to stir, drunken Violet getting restless.

Always looking for trouble, one of my foster mothers used to say. *Uncontrollable.* She might not have been so right at the time, but now she would be. Guess I turned out exactly like she thought—like all of them thought. That's not what I want to focus on. Something good. I want to focus on something good that's sitting right beside me.

Luke is staring straight ahead, arms folded, his muscles taut, his thinking face on, as if he's pondering some complicated theory on human nature and how we turn out the way that we do, what molds us into the people we are.

I shake my head. *God, I think some weird things when I'm drunk.*

Luke. Focus on Luke.

He's sitting close to me, but not close enough, so I scoot over and he shakes his head, his lips threatening to turn upward. "You have that look on your face," he says, turning his head toward me. "The one where I can tell you want to start trouble."

"You know me better than I thought," I say straightforward, not being able to see very clearly through the alcohol swishing around in my brain.

His eyes search mine confusedly. "Do I?"

I nod deliberately, a fire igniting in my chest based on lust. "And I bet you can guess exactly what I'm thinking right now." I move my hand down the front of my body, biting my lip as I touch myself.

He sucks in a slow breath and gradually lets it out, mouthing the word *wow*. He doesn't speak aloud, just wraps his fingers around my wrist, brings my hand to his mouth, and puts his lips around the cigarette I'm holding. It makes me think of his tongue and how good it felt when it was licking me earlier in the bedroom.

After he takes a drag of my cigarette, he lets me have it back then says, "You're thinking how awesome I am for winning three grand tonight."

"As awesome as that is, that's not what I'm thinking about." I shake my head, feeling the electricity in the air, the out of controlness, just the way I like it. Then I place the cigarette to my lips, not because I want to smoke, but because I want to tease him like he just did with me. I give it a good long suck, feeling a flicker of panic when I see Preston's face, the way it looked right before he shoved me down on my knees, turned on not just by getting a blowjob but by the pain and lack of desire in my expression. I quickly shove the mental images away and it gets absorbed by the vodka burning in my veins and clouding my mind and judgment. "So guess again," I say as I exhale a cloud of smoke.

Luke's eyes darken, shadows in the inadequate light flowing in from the lampposts, casinos and sights outside. He shifts toward me, his knee pressing against my leg as he cups his hand to my cheek and dips his lips to my ear. The warmth of his Bacardi laced breath caresses my skin and sends warmth throughout my body. *Safe. I feel that safeness again.*

"You were thinking about what I did to you in the bedroom a few hours ago," he says in my ear, his voice low and filled with desire, his breath hot against my skin. Sweltering—I'm sweltering and it's not from the heat of the desert. "And about how much you want me to do it to you again, only maybe slower this time and longer... take my time..." He has to be drunk as well and two drunken peas in a Challenger make for sporadic decisions without even a flicker of a thought about the consequences. And makes the adrenaline addict nearly fall into a state of euphoria.

Calmness overcomes me and settles inside my chest. I let my hands drift toward Luke's jeans, resting them right on top of his dick. Right there, in the backseat of the car with his uncle and cousin within earshot. And in return, Luke lets out a throaty groan that makes me want to rip off his clothes and scratch the shit out of him, like I was picturing doing back at the table.

But as my fingers start to wander up Luke's shirt, my nails gently scratching against his lean muscles, his uncle bursts the moment. "Okay, you two, let's wait until we get back to the house," he says with amusement. "I promise it's not that far."

I'm not one to get embarrassed, but either my cheeks heat or the air gets even hotter. Luke, however, looks completely unbothered as he sits back in the seat, putting his hands on top of mine so they're trapped inside his shirt, my palms pressed against his muscles and warm flesh. He gives me a look as if he has every intention to continue this right up the moment we get into the bedroom.

I just hope I can stay drunk enough that I can go through with it unemotionally, or I might have to find another alternative to settle the emotions buried inside, ones that want to burst out of me, both old ones and new ones. And I'm afraid once I let them out, I won't be able to put them back in again.

Chapter 11

Luke

Good guy? Bad guy? What kind of guy am I? A few months ago, I knew the answer and I was okay with that. Better to understand yourself than to be completely clueless. Not knowing is hard and right now, I'm the biggest, clueless asshole there is. Because I want to fuck the hell out of Violet. I want to fuck her long and hard until she screams out my name and stabs her nails into my skin, like she did in the car. God, that made me almost come inside my jeans, right here in the back seat.

I want her and need to take her more than anything. That's what the devil on my shoulder is whispering. On the opposite shoulder, there's this little angel, well, I guess that's what it is, but I can't be certain since I've never heard it before. It's telling me that Violet's drunk and hurting, and that it almost seems like she's trying to cover up her pain by doing reckless things she wouldn't necessarily do when she was sober. Like coming with me here, being with me, wanting me. It hurts to think about it like that, but I can see it in her eyes, the same look she had on the ledge when we were running from Geraldson. Only, I'm her ledge this time—her danger.

I go back and forth for the entire drive and come to the decision to be a good guy, but she makes it really complicated when we get back, stumbling into the bedroom together where she starts stripping off her clothes before I can even get the door shut. She's drunk enough that she's unsteady on her feet and sloppy with her movements. The way her eyes stay focused on me, though, is sexy as hell. First the dress, then the slip under the dress... and, oh hell, she has no panties on.

Before I can even take that all in, off goes her bra. She playfully throws it at me and it ends up hitting my face. I catch it, shaking my head, a smile starting to emerge; but the sight of her bare body in front of me makes me have to bite down on my lip to suppress a moan.

"You're seriously wasted." I drop the bra onto the floor, unable to take my eyes off her long, lean legs; flat, inked stomach; her perky nipples.

"So what? So are you." She backs up until her legs brush the bed and then she lowers herself down onto the mattress, crooking a finger at me to follow, waiting for me to go get her. And I want to badly, but I need to be a good guy, even if it's just once in my life.

"I'm always drunk," I admit truthfully, slowly crossing the room toward her. "You, on the other hand, usually

189

aren't." I stop just short of the bed where her legs are dangling over. "In fact, I've only seen you drunk once."

She gives me a blank stare. "Can you seriously tell me that you've never slept with a girl that was drunk before?"

I shake my head. "But you're different." I reach out and place my hand on her cheek, intoxicated enough that I don't give a shit how emotional I'm being. "And I don't want to sleep with you just because you're drunk and you're hurting over something... I want it to mean something... for both of us." I blow out a breath, my cock getting seriously angry with me. "But if you want to talk about it, we can. In fact, I wish you would."

She lets out a sharp laugh. "I don't want to talk at all." She leans away from my hand, her expression hardening and filling with panic. "Why are you trying to be all chivalrous right now, when hours ago you were so ready to fuck me?"

"Because I got caught up in the moment earlier," I tell her, letting my hand fall to my side. "And I'm not saying I don't want you. Trust me, I do, but I've just been thinking," I take a deep inhale and let it out slowly before I sit down on the bed beside her, "about how we haven't really talked about anything. And I know you don't want to, which is fine, but I just don't think we should sleep together. Not until we've confronted the stuff between us." God, this is a first for me. Naked girl in front of me, legs spread open, and I'm not willing to thrust my cock inside her.

I wait for her to get pissed at me, but she just starts breathing heavily as if she's struggling to get air into her lungs and her gaze is sweeping the room as if she's searching for a way out, this panicked, frenzy takes over the drunken look in her eyes. I'm not sure where it stemmed from so abruptly, but I know enough about panic attacks to know she's about to have one.

"Violet, relax." I put a hand on her knee, trying to get her to look at me. "I'm not going anywhere and I'm not going to make you talk about anything you don't want to."

Still breathing erratically, she looks down at my hand on her knee then wrenches her leg away from me. "Don't touch me." She jumps up from the bed and grabs the slip from off the floor, tugging it over her head. Then she starts for the door, ready to walk out. I get up to grab her, even though I know it's probably not a good idea to touch her when she's in this state of mind, but like hell am I letting her go out there in a piece of fabric that barely covers her ass and shows the outline of her nipples.

"Please calm down." I pause as her eyes land on me, wild panic flowing from them. I put my hands up, letting her know I'm not going to touch her. "I think you're having a panic attack."

"No, I'm not." Terror fills her expression as she looks from me to the door and then her gaze lands on the window. Without saying another word, she rushes to the win-window and throws it open, a hot breeze gusting in.

"Goddammit, Violet, stop it." I hurry to her, snagging her arm before she can climb out the window, panicking as I think of Amy. We're on the second floor and even though she could be okay jumping out, I'm not going to take that risk. "If you get dressed, then I'll let you go out the door... I just didn't want you walking out dressed in that."

"Let me go." She jerks her arm away from me, glaring at me. "That isn't what this is about." Then she swings her legs out of the window, but I grab the back of her dress and pull her to me. She fights against me, wiggling her arms and legs, writhing her body as I wrap my arms around her and pull her back to me. "Let me go... let me go..." she gasps, pushing back against me.

I rock her back and forth and kiss her head. "No, not until you tell me what's going on."

"There's too much..." Her voice cracks and even though I can't see her face, I think she's crying. "I need to turn it off..." She starts massaging her chest as if it's tender "It hurts..." Another gasp, then another.

I hug her against me, trying to figure out what I just witnessed and how to calm her down. I'm not sure if she was actually going to jump or if she was just thinking about it, but Jesus, what if she was? What if things are so bad she's ready to take pain over anything else?

"Please, let me go…" she begs between gasps, tearing my heart in half with the agony in her voice. "I just need to sit in the window for a moment… see it… and I'll be okay…" She tries to suck air in her lungs, but the anxiety is too great and I can tell she's not breathing very well.

She's going to blackout and I know I need to calm her down somehow, but I honestly have no idea how. When I get riled up like this, I either drink, gamble recklessly, or start fights. I want none of that for her, so I turn her around so she's facing me. She's too weak to really fight me, too focused on trying to breathe. Tears stain her green eyes and face, mascara running down her cheeks as she refuses to look me in the eye.

"Violet, look at me," I say in a soft but steady voice I'm pretty sure I've never, ever used before. I cup her face with one hand, while supporting her weight in the other. When she shakes her head, more tears streaming down her face, I try again in the gentlest voice I can summon. "Baby, look at me."

Her eyelids flutter as she tips her head up, the light reflecting in her glossy pupils. She makes eye contact with me, which is surprisingly intense, considering how exhausted she looks.

"I don't want to feel this way," she whispers, tears rolling down her cheeks. "I want to feel something else... not this... not all this pain... I don't even know where it came from. One minute I was drunk and then you turned me down and I..." she trails off, sucking in a breath.

"I'm so sorry, Violet, for causing you pain." God, kill me now. This is too much. Too unbearable, seeing her like this.

"Stop apologizing... It's not even your fault... it's your mom's... it's Preston's for making me do all that stuff... It's my own damn fault for not fighting him harder... for going back... for not just being able to let go of shit..." She starts to sob, and I wonder if she'll even be able to remember any of this in the morning. One thing's for certain, I sure as hell will, especially the part about Preston. "If you'd just let me near the window..." She inhales, forcing oxygen into her lungs as she opens her eyes to look at me again. "Just let me calm myself down... this will all be better." Her speech is a little slurred from the alcohol and it looks like she's fighting exhaustion, probably from the panic attack. I'm guessing if she was more alert and sober, then she'd not be openly admitting this to me.

"You want to jump out the window to make yourself feel better?" I choke on the idea of Violet hurting herself.

She shakes her head. "No, I just want to think about it... I need to feel the rush, not this." She puts a hand on her chest and presses her heart as if it's aching. "Please, Luke, just let me go and everything will be okay."

I shake my head. "No, I can't do that... ever..." My voice is strained as I stand us both to our feet and support most of her weight. Then, without saying anything, I pick her up and walk back to the window, not letting her go when I set her down, even when she climbs up in the windowsill and lets her legs hang down the other side.

It starts to make sense a little, bit by bit, piece by piece, how Violet never can seem to comprehend danger; at least, that's what I thought. But now, I get that she understands it; she just welcomes it. In fact, it seems to settle her down like booze and gambling does to me.

After what seems like a thousand deep breaths, she finally relaxes against me. "It's not the same with you holding me," she mutters, but she doesn't try to slip out of my arms or tell me to let her go. She just leans her head against my chest and I rest my chin on top of her head, holding on for dear life, praying to God we both don't fall.

Chapter 12

Violet

The first thing that comes to my mind when I wake up is that I can remember losing it. Completely and utterly losing it right in front of Luke. I was so drunk I didn't give a shit, even when he looked like I was scaring the crap out of him. When morning rolls around, it's a whole other story...

When I open my eyes and notice the heavy weight on my side. I realize that it's Luke's arm and that we're spooning in the bed, our bodies so close to each other there's no room for anything else. I've got my ass pressed against his manly part, which is gracing me with its morning wood. He's got his face pressed into the back of my neck, his warm breath caressing my skin and our legs are tangled together, the slip I have on riding up so I'm barely covered up at all and his hand is resting softly on my side. The smell of him overwhelms me and all I can think is, *please, just freeze this moment right here and never let me move forward or backward again.*

I'm surprised how content I feel, especially after the drama of last night. Maybe that's just denial. I don't want to admit that I got so trashed that I completely fell apart and he discovered my dirty, little secret. God knows what all I told him… I remember some stuff about pain… and Preston… dammit, did I tell him about the bruises and the blowjob?

I think about lifting his arm up and sneaking out before I can find out, finding the nearest bus stop and going home to avoid confrontation. Technically, though, I don't have a home, so it'd just be me going back to Laramie and trying to find a bench to sleep on until I can come up with an alternative living situation.

"How are you feeling?" Luke's voice dusts the back of my neck as he presses a soft kiss to my neck, right where my tattoos are, startling me.

My body twitches as he brushes my hair away from my shoulder and begins tracing gentle circles on it with his finger. "Fine, I guess," I tell him. "I have a little bit of a headache, but nothing a few pain killers won't cure." I force my tone to be light. Hopefully, he'll play along and pretend, let me stay in my land of make believe.

"What about the other stuff?" His hand slowly slides from my shoulder, down my side then rests on the side of my leg, bare skin to bare skin, his palm right over the bruises.

I squeeze my eyes shut and take several deep breaths before I can speak. "I'm not sure what to say… I'm sorry."

His hand tenses on my leg. "For what?"

I open my eyes and stare at the wall. "For turning all psychopath on you last night."

"You didn't go all psychopath on me last night. You had a fucking panic attack, which I totally get. Trust me. I've had my fair share of them." A pause, then his hand glides back up my body and neck, residing on my jawline. He turns my head toward him, forcing me to rotate my body with it so I'm facing him.

He looks so worn out, the circles under his eyes even more defined and his skin even paler than usual. He's shirt-less, the blanket covering just his bottom half so I can see his bare chest. He's still in shape and everything, but he looks like he's lost some weight. It's starting to concern me, like maybe he's not taking care of himself enough with his diabetes, but how do I bring it up to him?

"I want you to tell me what happened with Preston."

I shake my head, my lips trembling as I smash them tightly together, weak at just with the mention of his name. "I can't."

"I know it's hard," he says, his fingers spreading across my cheek. "But I need you to tell me… if he hurt you, I—"

I cover his mouth with my hand. "I don't want you hurting him," I state firmly. "And not because I care about him at all—I don't want *you* getting hurt." I wait a minute then lower my hand.

He's grinding his teeth in frustration. "If I promised you I wouldn't hurt him, would you tell me?" It seems like it takes a lot of self-control for him to say it.

He wants me to willingly talk about my problems? There's a new one.

"I hate talking about stuff aloud," I admit. "Don't you think it's so much easier just to keep stuff to yourself? Especially when you're the reason it happened it the first place? I mean, it'd be pretty pathetic for me to whine about anything that happened when I walked straight into it."

He considers what I said and then stuns me when I see a flicker of anger transpire in his eyes. "I used to think it was better to keep things bottled up, but I'm not so sure anymore. Not since I met you... And you running away, to Preston's, that wasn't your fault. Yeah, I wish you would have stayed... but completely get why you left."

"I should have came back after you called the police and turned your mom in... things would have been less horrible if I had," I mutter, swallowing hard, my mind racing with every bad choice I've made. "It wasn't like I fought him or anything. It was our deal while I stayed there." *Air in, air out. Breathe.* "He gives me a roof over my head and in return, I have to touch him… at least, that's what it was in the beginning. Then a week ago, I messed up a stupid deal and he got super pissed and kind of forced me down on my knees to…" I make a motioning gesture with my hand. "Well, you know. And that's where the bruises came from. I hit my leg on the bed when he was shoving me to my knees."

Luke's face turns from pale to red, his breathing quickening, his fingers going stiff on my cheek as if battling the urge not to ram his fist into something. I feel the need to add something.

"You can't get mad at him. In fact, you should be mad at me. I should have never gone back to him. I would have been better going and living out on the streets, but I was too scared to do that again and honestly, for some reason, I didn't want to be completely alone in the world yet and Preston is the only family I have, as fucked up as that is. I was weak and I know better than to let myself get that way." I shrug and continue, "The stuff that happens to me—the messes I get myself into—are my fault. In fact, it's kind of my thing. I'm careless and I don't think things through and this is where it's gotten me. Homeless, famili-less. And now I'm paying for my mistakes."

"You say that like you deserve it?" He's baffled, his anger fading to shock.

"Sometimes I don't think I do," I admit for the first time aloud. "I think about all the times I was moved from home to home. I always pretended that it didn't matter—that it was *them* not me. But I think it was more of a defense mechanism than anything… I could have tried harder to be a better child, but I was too stubborn and had too much rebellion in me."

He stares at me, his expression unreadable, one hand on my hip, the other on my face. I can feel his pulse throbbing through his fingertips. It seems as if he's searching for the right words, but I don't want him to say anything. I don't want to hear how he thinks that's not true, how I'm better than that, how it was everyone's fault but mine.

"I don't want a pity party," I tell him. "I was just saying my thoughts aloud."

"I wasn't going to give you a pity party," he replies, reminding me of the reason I was drawn to him in the first place. "I was going to say that when we get back to Laramie, I want you to stay with us." When I start to open my mouth to say… well, I'm not sure, he talks over me, "I'll sleep on the sofa and you can have the bedroom. Seth and Greyson will be completely fine with you being back. In fact, Seth even said something about missing you the

202

other day, but don't tell him I told you that." He pauses as if waiting for me to agree, but I'm not sure I'm ready for that yet. "And if you want, we can work out some kind of schedule where we don't have to be in the house at the same time, except for when we're sleeping."

It's amazing how easy it is to run away from your problems. Running back to Preston felt easier than going back to Luke. Yes, it has to do partly with who his mother is, but I think there was always more to it than that. I think it was easier to run away because it meant running away from what I was feeling. The night he told me who his mother was hurt so badly that I knew I was falling for him. Hard. I'd never had such powerful emotions toward someone before and that scared me.

"What about this thing with your... mother?" I ask, wincing as I remember the one and only night I met his mom, how crazy she looked as she sang that song with my parents' blood on her clothes. "What if something happens, like they arrest her? Won't that make things weird? More weird than they already are?"

He looks baffled, his jaw dropping, his eyes widening. "I fucking hope they arrest her. In fact, I've been waiting for them to my entire life."

Silence stretches between us as he drifts into thought. He rolls onto his back, his gaze floating to the ceiling while I examine his expression, trying to figure out what he could be thinking.

"How bad was it?" I dare ask. I've heard some stories from him—horrible stories—but I'm guessing there's more to it, more he hasn't told me. "With your mom, I mean... was it just the drug thing? Or was there something more?"

His breath catches in his throat, his eyes glued to the ceiling as he struggles with something internally. I'm about to tell him never mind, that he doesn't have to talk about it if he doesn't want to, but then he starts talking. "She used to like to play these games," he says, his voice faltering. "Ones that you'd never win, but you'd have to try or else you'd pay. There was one time she messed up the entire house and then told me to clean it, but the catch was that everything had to be put in the right place; otherwise I'd have to spend time with her... days... which should sound fun, but her idea of spending time together was not the normal mother/son relationship. More like a pet... only she liked the pet too much..." He squeezes his eyes and I wonder if he's trying to hold back tears. "You know, what really fucking sucks is that I just let her make me do all those things. Was I that afraid of her?"

"You were just a kid," I tell him. "It wasn't your fault."

"So. I knew what she was doing was wrong, but I didn't do anything to try to stop it because I was afraid of her—still am sometimes. A full grown man and just the sound of her voice makes me feel so angry and helpless."

Just like Preston does to me. God, we have so much in common. If only there wasn't that one thing, then maybe we could have something good.

He stays still for a while, while I wonder exactly what he's trying to say, read between the lines. His mother clearly hurt him, but it seems like there's so much more to it, way, *way* more. Dark things. Ones I should know. The things people do behind close doors—I've seen a lot of fucked up shit. However, I think Luke might have seen more, which is so sad it literally hurts my heart.

When he opens his eyes again, he rolls back toward me and starts grazing his finger across my cheek. "I'm sorry. I shouldn't be talking to you about this. You've been through your own shit and the last thing you need is for me to babble about my problems."

"It's okay. I asked you to," I say, battling to keep my voice. *Too many emotions, dammit. I can't keep doing this.*

I pause, inhaling and exhaling loudly, about to say something that I'd never thought I'd say aloud. "Luke…"

His hand stops moving on my cheek, his thumb tracing a line beneath my eye. "Yeah?" When I don't say anything right away, he adds, "You can say whatever you want to me, good or bad. I deserve whatever it is."

"I think I was wrong for leaving that day." The words fall from my lips and crash to the earth like fragile glass. Throughout the last two months, I'd thought it many times. Every time I woke up from my nightmares alone. Every time I saw a place Luke and I shared some kind of moment together. Every time Preston touched me… that's when I regretted my decision the most. But admitting that and letting everything go so I could get back to the place I was in before I left Luke, always seemed out of reach. What if it's right here, in front of me?

Just let it go.

The thought sounds like my father's voice, but the thing is, I didn't know him well enough to know if he'd be the kind of person who'd want me to hold a grudge or let it go. I was too young when he died, barely getting to know him and my mother. I want to believe, though, that they were good people, despite what anyone else says.

"You had every right to leave." He pauses, contemplating something, and then he suddenly sits up, taking his warmth with him. He rakes his hand through his hair. "You know what? I think I'm going to try to help them. After we go back, I think I'm going to pay her a little visit."

"I don't think that's a good idea." I hurry and sit up, stretching my legs that are still tucked under the blanket. "I don't want you being around her."

"I don't want to be around her either," he says in a tight voice. "And maybe if we can get her behind bars, I'll never have to again."

The idea of her being behind bars makes me feel better, but still, I'm not much of an optimist, so the concept that it will actually happen seems out of reach. "What about the other guy? Do you think she'll ever say who it is?"

He rotates on the bed, bringing his knees out from under the blanket. He's only wearing boxers and I can see pretty much all of him, including the massive bruise on his rib cage where Geraldson's bodyguard, or whatever that big guy was, hit him.

Luke puts his arm on his leg and leans close to me. "I'm not sure, but we'll figure this out. I'll do everything I can, but please tell me you're going to come home with me."

Home? Such a foreign word.

I don't agree—not ready to yet, but I want to and that has to be something. There's still so much between us that hasn't been said yet. And I could keep running and never have to talk about it, but the truth is I don't really want to anymore. I'm tired of running from everything and everyone. I've been doing it for almost fourteen years and maybe it's time to take a break.

***

After we talk for a little longer about lighter stuff, I realize that my phone battery died last night, so I find a charger and plug it in. There's a message from Detective Stephner telling me to call him back A.S.A.P., but when I dial him back, it goes straight to his voicemail again. I leave him another message and let the phone tag begin.

I take a nap while I'm waiting because apparently, between the energy I lost during the panic attack and the hangover, I'm exhausted. When I wake up, night has fallen and Luke is dressed to go out in jeans, a black shirt and boots, his hair done and his face freshly shaven.

He's lying down on the bed next to me, on top of the comforter and that notebook I saw him put into his bag back at the apartment is opened up on his lap, his eyes on the pages. Whatever is on there has got him worked up, his eyes glossy, his fingers trembling as he flips the page.

"Everything okay?" I ask, sitting up in the bed and stretching my arms above my head.

He jumps and presses his hand to his heart, startled. "Jesus, you scared the shit out of me."

I glance from the notebook to his wide eyes. "I can tell." I pause, looking down at the notebook again. "What are you reading?"

He shakes his head, closing the book. "It is... was..." He touches the leather band on his wrist that he always wears, tracing his fingers over the word *Redemption*. "My sister, Amy's, journal... my... mother sent it to me a few weeks ago." He sets the book aside, shaking his head. "I have no idea why she did it. I think it was another one of her games to try and get me to come home, like remember-ing Amy would tear me up enough that I would need to be with my mom or something." He rolls his eyes. "She's stu-pid, though. She had to of not read it because there's a lot of incriminating things in there about her that makes me want to never see her again." He pauses, conflicted, fid-dling with a small whole in his jeans. "Although she could have read it and was just too crazy to see how bad it made her look."

I'm about to say... well, something because it feels like I need to, but then he abruptly changes the subject.

"I'm glad you woke up before I left for the game. I wanted to talk to you about something."

I frown, bringing my knees up so they're under me, then smooth my untamed locks out of my face. "Why did you say it like that—like I'm not going?"

"Because you're not." He offers me this sexy, lopsided grin, as if dazzling me with his charm is going to make this easier on him. "I want—no, *need*—to make sure you're safe for the night."

"Don't try to smile your way out of this, Mr. Stoically Aloof," I say, raising my brows at him. "I want to go. Be useful. Not just sit around here and feel like I'm going to go crazy from the quietness." Something shifts in his expression, unravels, his tongue slipping out of his mouth to wet his lips. "What is it?" I ask, not sure if he looks upset or painfully relieved—perhaps both.

"It's nothing." He shakes his head, gaze glued on mine. "It's just that you used my nickname."

"So…" I'm so confused.

"So, I didn't think I'd ever hear it come out of your mouth again since you only use it when you're being flirty." He's right. I only used it when I was teasing him or trying to make him irritated because he looks sexy when he's frustrated, on the verge of losing it with me. "I've missed it," he adds, looking as though he's going to kiss me. And I want him to desperately, not just because with each kiss it feels like he's erasing more and more of Preston's kisses, but because when his lips are on mine, they're the only thing I can feel, my very own replacement to my adrenaline addiction.

"Aren't you going to kiss me?" I finally ask after a minute passes with him eyeing my mouth. I wince at the desperation in my voice, almost panting.

He cracks a smile, his eyebrows lifted. "Do you want me to kiss you?"

I remain indifferent. "Are you playing a game with me, Mr. Stoically Aloof?"

"If I was, I'd be winning." His lips quirk, amused. For an amazing moment, it feels like we're in the past again, challenging the crap out of each other. I don't want to lose and admit how much I want to kiss him, and neither does he.

Stubborn asshole.

"You want to know what?" I ask cockily, leaning in, my lips hovering over his. "I'll win this one." With that, I press my lips to his and give him a passionate kiss, my tongue enticing his lips open and meeting his as my arms encircle him and my fingers wander through his hair.

211

"How do you figure that was you winning?" he asks between kisses, his hand tangling through my hair.

I internally smile, almost laughing aloud at my brilliance. "Because I took the kiss from you."

He lets out this raspy chuckle then suddenly the kiss turns much more heated as he leans in toward me and him forces me back on my back, covering my body with his. "If that's the case then," his fingers slide up beneath the slip I still have on from last night, making their way up my leg, ready to enter me. Not wanting to give him the upper hand, though, I move my hand down and shove his fingers away, despite how much my body protests.

He lets out this growl, but before he can come at me again, I put my hand down his jeans and start rubbing him, making him pant, his body going rigid as I grip onto him and move my hand up and down.

"Dammit, Violet," he moans in my ear, nipping at my skin, teeth piercing and making those butterflies flutter in my stomach again. *Huh? I guess it wasn't the jager and vodka.*

With his body over mine, his arms struggling to hold up his weight, I stroke him, not even sure what the hell I'm doing, just going with it. No disgust. No shame. Just want. So much want.

I think he's about to reach the edge and I'm smiling to myself because technically, I sort of won; at least, in my head. But then someone knocks on the door and my hand instinctively pauses and Luke lets out a groan in protest.

"Luke, we gotta go!" his uncle hollers, pounding on the door again. "Or else we're going to be late and they won't let us in tonight."

"Just a second!" Luke shouts back, sounding pissed. His eyes shut and he presses his face to the crook of my neck as he grips onto the blanket, trying to calm himself down.

"Not just a second!" His uncle bangs on the door repeatedly. "We're already pushing our luck!"

Shaking his head, Luke grinds his hips against my hand one more time. "I'm going to fucking hurt him for this," he mutters. With another grunt of protest, he pushes away from me. My hand leaves his jeans and he adjusts himself as he sits up, looking like he's in pain.

"You okay?" I'm trying not to laugh, but it's difficult.

He narrows his eyes at me. "You think this is funny?" he asks, then slants toward me with a dark, hungry look on his face. I think he's going to kiss me, but then he says in a husky voice, "Just wait until I get back. I'm winning the next one." With that, he gets up, grabs his wallet from the nightstand, and tucks it into the back pocket of his jeans, looking pretty pleased with himself.

I roll onto my stomach and rest my chin in my hands as I stare at him. "You're really going to leave me here?"

"Well, I don't really have a choice anymore," he says, gripping the doorknob as Cole continues to knock on the door from the other side, chewing Luke out. "I have to go now, but I probably wouldn't have let you go anyway."

I give him a dirty look. "*Let* me go? Seriously? What is this? 1950?"

"No, I just care about you too much."

I get out of bed and cross the room to him, noting he looks a little pale again. I saw him give himself another injection this morning, so hopefully it'll help with his paleness and exhaustion. I don't know enough about diabetes though to know for sure. I'm starting to worry more and more though. I've seen him so drunk once that he needed my help checking his blood sugar and giving him pills.

"Fine, I'll let you *make* me stay here," I say, which gets him to smile. "Now go win big." I press my lips to his, giving him a quick kiss, then pat his ass. "That is how they do it on the football field, right?"

He shakes his head, trying not to laugh at me. "Please stay out of trouble," he says as he turns the doorknob.

Rolling my eyes, I give him a salute. "Yes, boss."

A thoughtful look rises on his face. "You should start calling me that more. I like it." I shake my head, and playfully pinch his side. He laughs and opens the door all the way.

Cole is standing there with his arms folded, looking annoyed, mad, and drunk, amongst other things. "I know I seem cool and everything," he says to Luke sternly, "but not with this. If I get you connections, you better follow through or else I'll drop you."

I can tell it irks Luke, and he probably has to bite his tongue really hard to stay calm. "Well, I'm ready now, so let's get going."

Cole glares at him then glances over his shoulder at me. "Ryler's staying if you want to go hangout downstairs with him."

I nod while Luke scowls at Cole. "I'll get dressed and head down." Then I wave at Luke and shut the door before he can freak out more.

I get dressed in a tank top and jeans, wishing I'd brought shorts, but didn't think it'd be this hot, before I go downstairs to see if I can stomach any sort of food. I haven't had too many hangovers in my life, yet I'm learning quickly that it makes my stomach super queasy.

When I get downstairs, Ryler is sitting at the kitchen table eating a sandwich, music playing in the background as he plays a game of solitaire. He seems really into it, twisting around one of his eyebrow piercings, lost in deep thought. When he notices me, he fights back a grin. *Feeling better?*

I sigh and make my way over to the table. "Yeah, sorry about last night. I get a little intense when I'm drunk."

You were fine. He flips a card over and then studies his next move. *Amusing more than anything.*

"Well, I'm glad you think so," I say then point to his plate. "Mind if I make one for myself?"

He nods, setting the cards aside and getting up. *I'll make you one.*

I shake my head and motion for him to sit back down. "Thanks, but I'm good." I open the fridge. "I'm totally self-sufficient."

He taps my side so I turn around and he signs. *Yeah, I can kind of see that.* He picks up the deck, but then looks like he wants to tell me something as I get out the mayo, lunchmeat, and cheese. Finally, he puts the deck of cards back down and I glance over at him. *So how did you learn sign language?* I tense and he must see it because he adds, *You don't have to tell me if you don't want to.*

"No, it's okay… I guess." I grab some bread from the loaf on the counter and a paper plate. "I learned it from one of my foster brothers." I don't look at him, not wanting to see his face when I reveal that I'm parentless, keeping my attention on making my sandwich. Mayo on bread, meat, cheese, topped off with more bread, and done. When I finally turn around with the sandwich in my hand, I discover he's staring at me.

His hands move in front of him. *I grew up in foster homes, too.*

I'm in mid-bite and it's a good excuse not to respond right away, but really I'm trying to pull myself together. This is a heavy subject that I don't like to talk about—my time spent being passed between families.

"How come?" I finally ask after I swallow the bite and sit down at the table.

Parents couldn't take care of me. It's signed so casually, yet I can see the pain emitting from his eyes.

"But you're with your dad now?" I pick some of the crust off the bread.

I know, but he didn't want me until I was eighteen and could pretty much take care of myself.

I feel bad for him. I lost my parents and was forced to live with other people. Ryler's parents gave him away by choice. "What about your mom?"

He shrugs. *Let's just say she was never ready to be a mom... then again, quite honestly, I still don't think my dad is ready to be a parent right now. He acts like a kid sometimes and is hard to trust... sometimes I feel like the parent.* He pauses, shaking his head at his own thoughts. *What about you? Where are your parents?*

I hesitate. God, how the hell did I end up in this conversation? "They died when I was five..." My voice cracks and I clear my throat.

I'm so sorry.

I shake it off and look for a subject change, getting so sick of hearing the word *sorry.* I know people mean well, but it doesn't change anything. "I like this song," I say, nodding at the iPod.

He gives me a questioning look, noting my need to change the subject, but lets it go. *Yeah, Taking Back Sunday is a good band. Great live, too.*

"I saw them once a couple of years ago," I say and then take another bite of the sandwich. "It was super badass."

We continue on about our favorite bands, but my lips are moving almost robotically, my parents taking up most of my thoughts. I just keep thinking about what it would be like if I ended up with them again, like Ryler with his dad? Of course, that can never happen, but sometimes it's good pretending, like I did for the first year or so after they died. It's actually the first time I've really thought about them without freaking out. Add the light conversation with Ryler and things are going pretty good. That is, until my phone starts vibrating madly inside my pocket. There must have been a delay when the battery died because a stream of text messages comes pouring in, times varying from last night to only hours ago.

Unknown: Been thinking about u a lot and how badly I want to hurt u.

Unknown: U think ignoring me is going to make me stop. Think again.

Unknown: This shit is getting old u little cunt.

Unknown: U disgust me, being with the son of the woman who took ur parents' life.

Unknown: U fucking whore. Text me back.

Unknown: Fuck u.

Unknown: If u don't text me back right now, some-thing bad is going to happen.

Unknown: I know u're in Vegas. Hope u have fun. I'll be waiting for u when u get back.

They end, just like that. It's not an ending for me, though, but a beginning of a panic attack if I don't find a way to calm down. He knows where I am, but the question is how? How did he find out when hardly no one knows I'm here? The only people who know I'm here are the ones with me… and Greyson.

"Shit." I jump from the chair, cutting Ryler off. He looks up at me worriedly, mouthing *what's wrong*. But I don't answer, dialing Greyson's phone number. It rings four times and then goes straight to his voicemail. I leave him a rushed message about calling me immediately.

He could be just at work, but what if he's not? What if something happened to him…? What if *unknown* is with him? God, I don't want to flip out, but I'm about to. Pins. Needles. Pins. Needles. They're poking madly underneath my skin.

"Can you excuse me for a second?" I ask Ryler and when he nods, I dash up to the guest room, unsure of what I'm going to do. At first, I'm only thinking about myself and about the many ways I could hurt myself, but then all my thoughts go to Greyson. I'm worried about him. Me—

Violet Hayes—worried about someone else besides herself. Actually, I'm worried about a lot of people at the moment.

I dial Greyson's number again, squeezing my eyes shut and holding my breath, crossing my fingers he'll answer. "Please, please, Greyson, pick up."

He doesn't though, so I end up dialing him ten times, over and over again, becoming like a stalker myself. Finally he picks up, but is very, very grumpy about it. I'm relieved to hear his voice all the same.

"What the hell, Violet?" he hisses in the phone. "I'm at work, filling in for you. Remember?"

"Shit. Sorry, but it's really important." I sit down on the bed and then lie back. "Did you tell anyone that I was coming to Vegas with Luke?"

There's some clanking and banging of dishes in the background. "Yeah, Seth. But that's it."

"Did he tell anyone?"

"Probably. He tells everyone everything." He pauses and I can hear the manager of the diner hollering something in the background. "Wait. Was I not supposed to say anything to anyone?"

"No, it's fine, but…" I waver, wondering if I should tell him what's really going on. I hate telling my problems

221

to people, but it doesn't seem like I have a choice anymore. "It's not really a big deal or anything, I've just been getting these weird texts and they know I'm in Vegas with Luke, which is strange since no one really knows except you and I guess Seth."

"Texts from that reporter again?"

"I don't think so. I mean, it could be a reporter, but I don't know." I let out a loud exhale. "Could you do me a favor and call Seth to see who he told, just so I can maybe get an idea of who's being a douche?"

"Of course," he says, not pressing any further. "Give me ten minutes and I'll take a break and go call him then call you right back."

"Thank you," I say, feeling the slightest bit lighter, the pins and needles not so potent and sharp. So this is what asking for help is like? I should really do it more often, but then again, getting to the point of asking feels like pulling teeth.

"You're welcome," he says, meaning it. "Talk to you in just a minute."

We hang up and I try to relax the best that I can, watching the minutes tick by, only breathing freely again when Greyson calls back.

"So it wasn't Seth," he says as soon as I pick up. "While I was talking to Seth on the phone, Benny over-heard me talking about it and said that some guy called the diner the other day, asking where you were."

My mouth droops to a frown. "You told Benny where I was?"

"Well, only because I was filling in for you. But Benny doesn't know you're with Luke, so I'm not sure how they found that out. Seth promises he hasn't said a word and he may be a gossiper but he's sure as hell not a liar. He's actually the opposite sometimes—too truthful."

"Yeah, I know." I sigh tiredly, wondering if the *unknown* is the one who called the diner. And why it matters to the guy enough to track me down? Who could he be? The other person there that night? Could it be fucking possible? The idea makes my hairs stand on end. "Thanks for finding that out."

"No problem." He hesitates then asks, "Everything going okay?"

"Yeah, I guess so." I force myself to knock down that wall again, the one I always try to first put up when people want to talk to me. "I got super trashed last night, though."

"That doesn't sound like you."

"I know. It was an impulsive decision that led to me crying myself to sleep while Luke coddled me... I feel like a crazy asshole. Seriously. I used to be so tough and badass and now I'm a hot mess."

"Everyone can be a hot mess sometimes. Trust me."

"Yeah, I know, but I hate making people *have* to take care of me."

"I'm sure Luke didn't mind, Violet," Greyson assures me. "In fact, he probably kind of enjoyed it, seeing as how he's in love with you."

"We've had this conversation way too many times," I remind him. "Luke's not in love with me. We just have... well, I don't know what we have, but it sure as hell isn't love."

"You sure about that?" he questions cynically. "Because I think you just don't want to admit that he is because you're afraid—afraid of letting someone feel that way about you."

"Yeah, I'm sure, Mr. Therapist," I utter quietly. "Besides, I don't even know what love is."

Silence stretches between us, the awkward kind. We've talked a lot, but I'm usually pretty closed off, so I think my openness about my emotions shocked him. "Violet, I—"

I cut him off. "Hey, can I call you back? Luke just walked in." A lie, but I'm not ready to have this conversation with Greyson yet and probably never will be.

"Yeah, sure." He seems hurt, like he knows I'm bullshitting him, which shows how much he knows me. "Call me back, though, okay? I worry about you."

"Yeah, absolutely," I say and then quickly hang up, my heart racing inside my chest as I fight to catch my breath.

"I don't even know what love is? Really, Violet? I need to start keeping my damn mouth shut," I mumble to myself, sitting down on the edge of the bed and letting my head fall into my hands. For a brief instant, I try to remember what it felt like to be loved by my parents, what it felt like to be hugged, cared for, feel warm on the inside instead of hollow and cold. Surprisingly, my thoughts drift to Luke and when he calmed me down last night, right in the middle of a panic attack. No one has ever gotten me to do that before, or better yet, has even tried to calm me down.

As I'm lying there, trying to sort through my emotions without wanting to fling myself out the damn window, my phone vibrates from inside my pocket. I think it's my stalker texter, but then I realize the phone is actually ringing this time. When I see Detective Stephner's name flash across the screen, relief washes over me as I answer it.

"It's about damn time," I say to him as I put the phone up to my ear. "I was beginning to think you were intentionally avoiding my calls."

"I've been busy." Something in his voice throws me off a little. It's not that he's being rude so much as he sounds anxious.

I sit up straighter. "Busy with what exactly?" I ask curiously.

"I can't tell you yet, not until we know for sure," he tells me with a hint of remorse. "But as soon as I can, I will."

My heart hammers deafeningly and I'm seriously starting to worry it's going to leap straight out of my chest. "Is it about my parents? Did they find evidence against Mira? Or did they find the other person who did it?" My words are rushing out of my lips a hundred miles a minute as the possibilities stream through my head. Is this it? The moment I've been waiting for? Is justice finally going to happen after all these years?

"Violet, calm down," he says like it's something so easy to do. "I can't officially discuss anything yet, but like I said, as soon as I can, I'll call you."

"That's not fair," I gripe. "You shouldn't have called me until you could talk to me."

He sighs tiredly. "I called because you called me, re-member? You left a message about getting some texts again."

"Oh yeah." The adrenaline surging through me makes my voice uneven. "At first, I thought it was another report-er, but they know stuff about me that a reporter wouldn't unless they were stalking me."

"Give me the details," he says and I start yammering off what's been going on and even read him all the texts.

"Can you forward those to me?" he asks when I'm fin-ished yammering. "I'd like to have a copy."

"Of course," I reply, already on it. "You'll get them in just a second."

"I want to put a trace on your phone, too," he says as I put the phone on speaker so I can still hear him, but work the message section. "See if we can track the number the texts are coming from."

"It comes up as unknown, though."

"Doesn't matter. It could still be traceable."

"How long will something like that take?"

"It all depends. I'll get working on it as soon as we hang up. And if you get any more texts, call me immediate-ly." He gives a reluctant pause. "Violet, I have to ask about

Luke. Are you really with him right now like the texts are saying?"

"Yeah… it kind of just happened." I suddenly feel guilty about it, especially with the way he says it, like he's disappointed. "There was some stuff going on and… Look, I know who his mother is and everything, but he's not a bad person."

"I never said he was," he states. "I was just wondering where he was in case we need to get ahold of him for some reason."

"Oh." I give another long pause, knowing there's no point in asking, but I can't help it. "Can't I have like a tiny detail about what's going on?"

"I'll try to call you in the morning," he disregards my question. "And make sure you're with someone at all times. I don't want you wandering around by yourself until we figure out where these texts are coming from."

"Okay, I will," I tell him, frustrated that he still won't spill the beans about whatever's going on, even though, deep down I know he can't without getting into some serious trouble.

"Good." He hesitates then adds, "And, Violet, just try to relax. I have a feeling some good things are going to be happening soon."

I think it's his way of giving me a hint, that whatever's going on is a good thing. At least, that's the way I'm choosing to take it. And by the time I hang up with him, I feel a little lighter, like maybe soon I'll be able to breathe again without the weight of life pushing down on me, for the very first time in almost fourteen years.

Chapter 13

Luke

Things were going good. So, so good. Violet and I were finally talking and I felt like she was really opening up to me. But I should have known it wouldn't last. You'd think I'd have learned my lesson after all this time, but I guess I'm a slow learner. Shortcuts. There's always risk when it comes to them.

The good day had been plummeting to begin with the more the hours went on. It started out when I was reading more of Amy's journal and found something so fucked up, I couldn't even process it—the reason Caleb raped her. And reading about it nearly tore me to shreds.

I was never supposed to find out about it, my sister Amy had wrote across the lined paper, the black ink smeared as if she'd been crying and the tears had dripped down to the pages. *The rape was supposed to be part of the deal. My mother owed a debt to him for drugs and had offered me to Caleb against my will and Caleb had more than gladly took up the offer, but only if he could have sex with me without my consent. Just like that, my mother sold her daughter, like a pimp sells a prostitute.*

I was at a party when it happened. I remember Caleb had his eyes on me the entire time, everywhere I went that night, and it bothered me enough that I left the party early and went home. I knew his reputation that he liked to be rough with girls, get them drunk and take advantage of them. He also sold drugs to my mother—I remember thinking that a lot that night and how sad it was because he was so young to be in so deep. My mother, well, she hadn't always been that way, not until my father took off and then she kind of went off the deep end, getting high all the time, her mind slipping further and further away from her. I think she might have had an underlying mental disorder to begin with and all the crack and heroin just made it worse.

Maybe that's what Caleb's problem was, because why would someone ever want to do that to another person? Why would he want to follow me down the hallway and grab me from behind... when I tried to scream, he covered my mouth with his hand. All the lights were off in the house and Luke's door was shut, so he couldn't hear my muffled cries as he dragged me toward my room. But my mom could—she could see me when she walked out of her room, the light blinding behind her as she peered into the hallway right before Caleb got me inside my room. She'd been wearing her robe and had this weird look on her face, relief maybe.

231

"Be quiet," she'd told Caleb as she'd tied up her robe. "I don't want you waking up her brother." Then she'd turned back into her room, closed the door, and let Caleb drag me into my bedroom, gag me and tie me up, then rape me over and over again until every part of me died inside.

My soul died that night and I'm hoping that my body will soon follow because being here is just too hard... too painful.

I was about in tears when I'd finished reading it, but Violet had woken up and I forced myself to pull it together. I noticed the date in the entry of the corner when I was shutting the notebook. Two days before Amy took her own life because she couldn't deal with the idea of living anymore in the darkness that had taken over her mind.

It made me want to throw up. How could my mother do that to her own daughter? But the real fucked up thing was that I wasn't even as surprised as one might think and it makes me worry just how many 'surprises' are in store for me in the future.

Thankfully, through all of this, I managed to keep my shit together long enough to get me out of the house and away from Violet. I'd left the house, thinking things couldn't possibly get worse, until Uncle Cole up and decided that he wanted to cheat, too, and without warning me.

The bosses of The Warehouse caught on to what we were doing and I guess it wasn't the first time it happened with Cole.

That's when they came down and dragged him toward the back room. I'm right in the middle of a winning hand and just like that, there's all this commotion. Cole puts up a fight as two guys grab an arm and pull across the open warehouse.

I'm getting to my feet, trying to figure out what to do, whether I should go after him, when a large, overweight guy with a thick neck, dressed head-to-toe in black comes up to me.

"Follow me," he orders and when I hesitate, adds, "It'll be worse if you don't."

Grinding my teeth, I set the cards down on the table and follow the guy as he makes his way past the poker tables toward this back area hidden behind a steel wall. By the time I get there, the two guys that hauled my uncle off are beating the shit out of him, one holding him by the arms while the other rams their fist into his gut, face, arms— everywhere.

"Hey," I start to protest when I'm shoved face first to the floor by a heavy set of hands and end up bashing my face on the concrete. The taste of blood fills my mouth and my jaw starts to throb as I go to push to my feet, but a foot comes down and holds me in place. They take my wallet out of my pocket—I'm sure to take all the cash I have in there. It's not everything, but it's enough that I'm in deep trouble. Not too mention all I won tonight is gone.

"And if you come back here again," one of the guys says to Cole as he slams his fist right into his face, blood spurting from his mouth, "Greford won't let you walk out of here."

The foot moves from my back as they let go of my uncle and he falls to the floor, unable to even hold his head up. I push up and start to head to him when one of the guys comes at me.

I shove him back roughly. "Don't even fucking think about it. This has nothing to do with me."

"Oh, you think so," the guy says snidely. He has this gnarly scar going down his eye and this sick look in his eyes as he wipes some of my uncle's blood off his chin. "You come here with a cheater, you're declared a cheater. Rules of the game." Then he cranes his arm back and punches his fist into my jaw, right on the side that hit the concrete.

Instinctually, I react with a ram of my own fist, hitting him right in the side. It shocks him a little and then suddenly I'm being held back and the scarred guy sucker punches me three or four more times before I'm let go.

My whole body hurts, but the pain is minimal to the reality of the situation. My uncle's unconscious, no money, no way to pay Geraldson back.

"Now get your damn asses out of here," Scarred guy says and then spits on the floor in front of me before leaving with the other guys.

Stumbling to my feet, I stagger my way over to my uncle, bruised, beaten and broken, ready to give up. When I roll him over, he looks dead—bloody, face swollen, nose a purplish blue. But then he opens his eyes and gives a cough.

"Well, damn. That sucks." No apology. No excuses. No nothing.

Annoyed and sore as hell, I help him to his feet and get him to the car. He gives me the keys, unable to drive with one of his eyes swollen shut. I hop in the driver's seat and drive back toward the house, my mind racing a million miles a minute.

Fuck, I'm fucked. This is the thought that's running over and over in my mind as I drive.

"Should I… should I maybe take you to the emergency room?" I finally ask, feeling my own body ache with the need to be treated.

He shakes his head, turning toward the window, mumbling, "There's a warrant for my arrest and the last thing I want to do is get caught."

"For what?" I ask, merging onto the freeway.

"That's none of your business." He rests his head on the window and stays silent for the rest of the drive.

After we get to the house, I help him inside and can't help but think of my own future and wonder if this is where I'm headed. Twenty-years-old and I've already had my ass kicked more than I can remember for getting caught cheating. And now I have no money to payback Geraldson. I'm wondering if that's how Cole was. From what I can remember, even when I was five-years-old—he would have been twenty—he was gambling, drinking, and fighting, the same way he is now.

By the time we stumble into the foyer, it's late, well past midnight. There's a lamp on in the living room, but the rest of the house is dark, so I make my way in there, Cole's arm around my shoulder as I bear most of his weight with my own battered body.

"Easy," he mutters to me as I maneuver us down the step and through the doorway toward the sofa.

When we enter, Ryler, who's sitting on the couch watching television, instantly looks over at us. He sets his beer down and doesn't seem the least bit shocked at the sight of us, only annoyed at the sight of his father and the condition he's in. Cole looks even worse than earlier. All of the places he was hit are now swollen up twice as bad as when we left The Warehouse. Ryler signs something short and simple, his movements clipped.

"Hey, you were the one who decided not to go tonight," Cole gripes as he slowly lowers himself down onto the chair beside the sofa and slips his arm off my shoulder. "You know I do these things when you're not around—I can't help myself."

Ryler glances from me to his father then signs something again and even though I don't know sign language, the movements of his arms are enough for me to tell he's said something harsh.

"Hey, Luke asked me to help him," Cole protests, touching his puffy cheek with his fingertips and wincing. There's blood splattered all over his torn shirt and I'm fairly certain his nose is broken. "That's what I was trying to do. If I wouldn't have got caught, then Luke wouldn't have had to share his winnings with me and would have had enough to pay his debt."

"I didn't ask you to do that," I tell him, not wanting to be rude, but I don't want the blame for this, nor did I ever want to lose all my money and be back to square one. "I would have been fine with playing another night or two. Now I have nothing and no game to go to."

"I'll find us another place," Cole promises, reclining back in the chair and putting his feet onto the table. He's lost his shoes somewhere—who knows where, though. "I just need a few days." He shuts his eyes and lets his head tip back.

"I don't have a few days." I rub my hand down my face and wince, forgetting that my cheek is injured. "I'm so fucked."

"We'll figure it out. Nothing I haven't handled before," Cole mumbles while Ryler shoots a glare at his dad and throws the beer cap at him to get him to open his eyes. When he does, Ryler mouths something, but I can't catch what. "Hey, I'm good at figuring stuff out under pressure," Cole tells Ryler then looks up at me. "You think maybe you could ask your dad to spot us some cash so we can get things moving again?"

I shake my head and back out of the room. "I'm not asking my father for anything."

He frowns. "Luke, it might be our only option."

I hate the way he says *our* option, as if his problem has become my problem. "I have enough problems of my own," I tell him. "I don't need anymore."

"Just think about it," Cole says while Ryler shakes his head, aggravated, as if his father does this all the time and Ryler is tired of it. "I'm sure he would do it for you if you asked him."

Even if I wanted to ask him, I'm not so sure he would or if he has access to that kind of money. I don't want to go down that road with my father anyway, so it's not an option.

"I'm leaving tomorrow morning," I tell Cole then leave the room. He calls out my name, almost panicking, but I know it's not over me. It's over himself. He's a gambling addict. Pure and simple. My possible future, if I don't figure out a way to straighten my act up.

What a wakeup call. Although, I'm not even sure if it's what just barely happened, or if it had something to do with finding out the truth about what happened to Amy, or if it was Violet opening up to me and making me want to be a better person.

As I tiredly drag my sore ass up the stairs, I try to remember how I got to this point in time, how I messed up my life so badly. Tired. Beat up. Broke. Alone. The last one might not be so true. That's really up to Violet and whether she'll ever have me again. Honestly, she'd be better off without me, at least until I clean my act up, but I'm too selfish to walk away from her.

That's what I'm trying to convince myself not to be— selfish—when I enter the room and see her lying in bed, the covers kicked down, wearing one of my shirts, her long legs stretched out. I realize I need her. Through the insanity of my life, Violet is the one sane thing I have, even if our relationship is insane itself.

She's left a lamp on, so there's a soft trail of light in the small room. I tug my shirt off and then slip off my boots as I make my way to the bed, pausing when I get beside it to unbutton my jeans and take them off. Her back is to me, her head resting against the pillow, her hair lose and down her back. I reach forward and brush it aside then trace my fingertips along the two stars on her neck, her skin so soft and familiar, everything I want.

I can barely remember the first time I ever had sex and all the times after are a blur until I met Violet. Sure, it always felt good, for me at least. Not sure about the women since I didn't care nor did I stick around long enough to ask. There was something about having that kind of control over a person like that—where I could just walk away before they ever used me—that made me feel briefly content. It would always fade though and I'd only get the contentment again when I fucked the next one and so on and so on. I've never actually been with anyone more than once, including Violet, but not because I used her and bailed like with the rest of the women I've been with.

Violet has always been different from anyone else I've been with. I knew that from the first moment she literally fell into me. At the time, I didn't know what exactly made her different or why I had the sudden need to be around the same woman for more than an hour. Now, I think I know.

Because I'm in love with her. I just can't tell her that. Not yet. I'm not ready and neither is she. In fact, I'm not sure she'll ever be ready for that, not with me, but I want to stick around and find out—be there for her.

Sucking in a deep breath over this terrifying revelation to myself, I climb into the bed and press up against her, wrapping my arms around her, slipping one underneath the crook of her neck so her head is resting on my arm like a pillow. I feel her jump a little and I half expect her to wake up out of her nightmare and be in panic, like she normally is whenever she wakes up, but she must have been awake the entire time because she barely stirs before she relaxes against me.

"You smell like cigars," she mutters as my fingers drift up and down her side. "And beer."

I pull her closer against me and breathe in her scent; something vanilla with a hint of perfume that makes me briefly shut my eyes and get lost. "You look good in my shirt," I whisper, opening my eyes. I sweep her hair out of the way and kiss the sensitive spot on her neck, right below her jawline, letting my lips linger there to taste her skin.

"Luke…" She almost sounds torn, her fingers finding my arm and digging into my skin. I wait for her to pull away, stop us from doing something, but then her back curves in and her ass presses against my cock.

The contact of it makes me groan and bite down on her skin more roughly than I intended on doing. In response, her nails dig into my skin, her back arching even more as my knee slides between her legs and I slip my hand up underneath her shirt to grip her hip, her skin warm.

"God, you feel so good…" I trail off as I start sucking on her neck and rubbing my knee against her while she begins rocking her hips with my movements, causing my cock to go rock hard. I could seriously be content with this, just touching her, and it's frightening that I don't need to take more, even though I want it. Need is so much different than want. Need is something driven by an addiction while want is something *I* want do to. Want. I want Violet.

She must think the opposite, though, because suddenly she's slipping out from my hold. My eyes widen as she moves away from me, but then she turns around, climbing on top of me and straddling my waste. Reaching for the collar of her shirt, she yanks it over her head and tosses it onto the floor, strands of her red and black hair falling to her bare shoulders. She's not wearing a bra or panties and when her nipples hit the air, they instantly get hard, which makes my cock instantly get more eager.

"Fuck, baby, I..." I trail off as she helps me slip my boxers off and then returns to my lap. I've never had a girl take control like this. Usually I'm the one that needs the control. And it's hard not to grab her and flip her over, take things over, but I manage to stay put beneath her and see where this goes.

A small smile touches her lips as she places her hands on my shoulders and pins me down to the mattress. "I think you were going to say something along the lines of, I win." Then she reaches down and grabs my jeans from off the floor. Before I can ask her what she's doing, she sits back up and puts a condom down on my chest.

"How did you know one was in there?" I ask, picking up the condom.

She shrugs, brushing her hair out of her eyes. "I just assumed."

I frown. "You know I haven't been with anyone since you, right?"

"I wouldn't blame you if you had," she says. "We weren't together."

"Well, I haven't." And it's the truth. Sure, I've thought about messing around, taking my mind off stuff, but going through with it was too hard and always thinking of Violet would put an end to it before things ever got too far.

"I guess you're a little deprived then." She rocks her hips, rubbing her wetness against my cock. Jesus, I swear she knows exactly how to get under my skin in the best fucking way possible.

Something snaps inside me, something that I've never felt before. And I feel even more helpless when she starts to lower herself down on me, slipping my dick inside her. Halfway down, I can't take it anymore and with one hard thrust, I slam my hips against her and thrust my cock deep inside.

She immediately winces and bites down on her lip, her muscles tightening around me. I freeze, suddenly remembering that she's only had sex once, and that was two months ago. She's still tight as hell and I was rough. Really, really fucking rough.

"Shit, did I hurt you?" I ask, sweeping some of her hair out of her face as her fingernails stab into my shoulders.

She shakes her head, the pain in her expression shifting to pleasure as she rolls her hips. "No… it feels good, just a little intense… it's been awhile…" She repeats the rolling movement over and over again with her hips, going slowly, as if she's savoring the sensations, her hands going to her shoulders and she runs her fingers down her body.

It's driving me crazy, watching her eyes gloss over, her lips parted as she presses down on me, touching herself, totally in control. Finally, I lose it again and start moving with her, thrusting my hips upward, my hands finding her waist and holding on. I move slow at first, but then get faster, harder, rougher the more she moans. Her head starts to fall back and I sit up, still holding onto her and moving. I press my lips to hers and she kisses back briefly, but is so lost in the moment, she ends up biting down on my bottom lip.

"Harder," she gasps, pressing against me as I rock into her, our movements matching perfectly. "Oh God… please… harder…"

I'm terrified beyond imaginable. Seriously. I can't think about anything else but her. Every single part of me belongs to her at that moment. I feel something change inside me, something that makes me want to be a better person forever.

I love you, I want to say.

My problems are momentarily forgotten. Life is momentarily forgotten. And all I can do is hold on and hope I never have to let go.

Violet

Holy hell, this is way, way better than the first time I had sex. Less painful. More intense. But I think that might be because Luke is letting go more this time, instead of being careful with me.

I'm on top of him, clutching onto his shoulders, while he sits up and thrusts in deep, the movement of my hips matching his. One of his hands is gripping at my waist, while the other rests at the base of my neck, putting gentle pressure against my flesh as he holds onto me and kisses me with so much passion I can barely breathe.

We keep moving and moving, getting more lost in each other, our skin beading with sweat as we become breathless, exhausted. It feels way too good to stop—I never want it to stop. And he seems to feel the same way, too, savoring each kiss, grip, bite, each brush of our skin and uniting of our bodies until we both fall helplessly into bliss at the same time.

I cry out in sheer pleasure, the sound of my voice unrecognizable as my fingers stab at his skin in desperation, needing to hold onto something. Luke keeps thrusting into me a few moments longer before he starts to slow, pressing one last time deep inside of me as his head collapses against my chest.

He remains still for a while, breathing heavily against my chest, like he's afraid to move. I kind of don't want him to either because everything feels perfect right now, which is rare for me, if nonexistent. Eventually, he shifts back down, slipping out of me, but bringing me with him and pulling me against him as we lie in the bed, face to face.

As the lamp cast the light over his cheek, I realize there's a massive lump there, on top of a preexisting bruise and a little bit of dried blood. I'd been so caught up in the intimate moment I hadn't realized it was there until now.

"What happened?" I ask, gently placing my hand over the injury. "Did you get in a fight?"

He shrugs, eyes on mine as he leans into my touch as if my hand is soothing him. "A little one, but nothing too major."

"Did you get caught cheating?"

His breath falters from his lips. "Cole did, but it's not that big of a deal. I don't owe any money or anything." His voice is off pitch and all that peace we had moments ago shatters into a million pieces I so want to put it back together again.

"They took the money, didn't they?" I ask with a frown.

He doesn't answer my question, only uttering, "I'll figure something out." He blows out a tired breath and then rubs his eyes, appearing worn out.

"I want to help," I tell him, tracing the lines of one of his tattoos on his rib cage. There are actually several tattoos on him and he told me once that he went through a phase where he'd get a tattoo every time he felt shitty, which meant he felt shitty a lot. "Let me help."

"I'm not going to let you deal drugs to help me," he says in a clipped tone, shaking his head. "I'd rather get the shit beat out of me than have you do that and owe *him*." His expression softens a little as he puts a hand on my back and gently sketches his finger up and down my spine. "Let me sleep on it. I might have an idea, but I need to figure out how desperate I am."

I don't know what his idea is, but it worries me because the last time I saw that look of pure helplessness on his face was the night he told me that his mother could possibly be my parents' killer.

Chapter 14

Luke

I watch her sleep for most of the night, thinking. My head so cluttered I can barely breathe. By the time I'm actually finished with a thought-out plan, the sun is coming up and I've had absolutely no sleep. It's been that way for the last couple of months and between that and the drinking, I'm starting to feel the effects of it on my body. Constantly tired, I wonder how I'm ever going to survive football season if I don't get my act together.

My act together. It seems like I have so much to do before that can ever be possible, but as I lie here looking at Violet asleep in my arms, I want to do it more than anything.

As the sun rises higher and lights up the room, I decide to take the first step, even though I don't want to at all. I begrudgingly get out of bed and grab my phone to make a call I never thought I could make in a million years. The alternative—staying here until I can figure something else out—isn't something I want to do anymore.

It's still early in California, but my dad answers after three rings. "Luke, is everything okay?"

I swear to God it's like he knows I need something. "Not really." I pause, waiting for him to say something, but he doesn't as I stare out the window. "Look, I need a favor... I need to borrow some money." If he turns me down again, I don't think I can ever ask him for anything.

"Okay." He already sounds wary. "How much do you need?"

I glance over my shoulder as Violet stirs in the bed, then make my way over to the bathroom attached to the room and go inside so I don't wake her up. "Nine grand."

He lets out a slow, low whistle. "Shit, Luke. That's a lot of money."

"I know it is." I shut the door, recline against it, and slide to the floor. "I wouldn't be asking if it wasn't an emergency."

"Are you in some kind of trouble?"

"You could say that." I hesitate, not sure I want to tell him, not wanting to give him the right of knowing me yet, but then suddenly, there's all this pressure inside my chest and it explodes without warning. Everything comes pouring out of me. And not just the gambling part. I tell him how much I drink. What happened between Violet and I. Everything my mom did. Even what I found in Amy's journal. And by the end, I'm crying, like a scared, little boy. It

251

makes me feel so pathetic. So weak. So out of control, like when I lived with my mother. Part of me hates myself, but the other part feels relieved, like I can breathe again.

"Luke, we're going to fix this," my dad says after I finally stop sobbing long enough for him to speak again.

"You can't fix it," I say, sucking back the tears. "Not most of it anyway."

"Well, I'm going to fix what I can," he tells me so calmly I don't even know how he's doing it. I just piled on twenty years of baggage onto him and he's cool as can be. "And the rest we'll figure out together." He pauses as if he's collecting himself. "The first thing I'm going to do is wire you the money. You can head back to Laramie and it should be there by the time you get there. Then you'll pay back this Geraldson guy."

I wipe the tears from my eyes with the back of my hand. "And then what?"

"And then I want you to come visit me," he says and before I can protest, he adds, "Just for a week, so we can talk and maybe get to know each other a little bit better... I'd like to get to know my son."

"You think talking is going to help?" I question skeptically. "Because I'm not so sure."

"I think it's a step… and if you'll let me, I'd like to take that step with you and hopefully more steps." He sighs. "I know I haven't been there for you and I can't make up for the past," now he sounds like he's choking up, "but I'd like to try my damn hardest. You just need to let me try."

"I have football practice starting in a couple of weeks," I say. "And classes. It's hard for me to go somewhere right now."

"Can you take some time off?" he asks, hopeful. "Just a week or so."

"I hate taking time off. And I've already missed more than I'm comfortable with." I'm being a pain in the ass, still uneasy about the whole thing. Well, more like frightened. When I was younger, it was all I thought about all those times during the needles, hugs, petting, madness—that he would come back and save me. However, he never did and I nearly rotted to death in that house. And now, it's hard to let that all go.

"Then I'll come to you," he insists determinedly. "If you say it's okay, I'll fly out there and see you."

I run my hand over my head, letting out a stressed breath. "How long would you stay?"

"As long as you want me to," he replies. "I'd take a few hours at this point."

"That's a far flight for a couple of hours."

"No, it's not." The way he says it makes me want to cry again, but I suck the tears back before they spill out.

"Fine, you can come out if you want." I push myself to my feet. "And you can stay for a few days."

It takes him a second to respond and when he finally does, I can tell he's crying but trying not to let me hear it. "Good. I'm so glad. I'm so, so glad."

It feels so strange and unbelievable, letting stuff go that I've been carrying around forever. I just hope that it all works out, but I'm not holding my breath just yet.

Chapter 15

Violet

When I wake up, Luke's not in the bed and I have this strange moment where I flip out, not just because Luke isn't there beside me but also over the way I wake up. My usual gasping ritual from my nightmares is absent, instead my eyes simply opening and all I can think is: *What the hell?*

It's more frightening than anything. I've been waking up that way and now suddenly I'm not. It feels like a part of me has gone missing and I don't know what to do with it.

And then my text goes off and makes things worse.

Unknown: Why did you call the police? U fucking cunt. You're so dead.

I'm trying not to flip out as I read the message over, when Luke walks out of the bathroom. I take one look at him, though, and the problem gets lost. He's still in his boxers, his hair ruffled, his jaw scruffy, and his eyes are red and puffy—either he's stoned or he's been crying. I'm guessing it's the latter.

"What's the matter?" I sit up quickly, the blanket falling from my chest. I'm still naked from last night and his gaze drifts to my chest, but only for an instant then he rubs his eyes and sighs.

"I called my dad." He stares down at the floor, a crease at his brow, confused. "I couldn't think of anything else to do, so I called him and asked him for the money."

"What'd he say?" I know very little about Luke and his dad's relationship, other than they don't have one and Luke has had no interest ever in having one with him because of his absence during his childhood, so if he asked him for help then it's a huge deal.

He scratches at the back of his neck, exhaling before looking at me. "He said he would, but I have to let him visit me."

I set the phone aside on the nightstand and swing my legs over the edge of the bed. "He blackmailed you?"

"No, not really. He just said he'd give me the money and that he wanted to come see me and I kind of just agreed." He sits down on the bed beside me. "This is so weird."

Not knowing what else to do, I scoot closer and rub his back. "I'm sorry, but I'm glad he's helping you, instead of you trying to gamble again." My words are shocking. Usually, I crave danger, but I'm discovering that if danger means Luke getting hurt it's not thrilling at all.

"Yeah, I guess I am too." He lowers his head into his hands. "But we'll see how it goes. I'm not going to go into this hopeful or anything." He sits for a while with his head down, breathing softly—I think he might be trying not to cry.

I stay quiet and keep rubbing his back until finally he raises his head back up, trying to discreetly wipe the tears away from his eyes. He clears his throat a few times and then gets to his feet, grabbing a pair of jeans from his bag. "I think we should get going," he tells me. "The last thing I want to do is stay here with Cole. The guy is in way worse than me," he pulls his jeans on and does up the button, "which says a lot."

I nod, then climb out of bed and go over to my bag, his eyes following me the entire way. "I'm actually anxious to get back, too," I say, grabbing a shirt and pair of black pants. "I talked to Detective Stephner last night and even though he wouldn't tell me anything, I could tell there was something going on with the case." I slip on the jeans. "I'm hoping it's good."

"When will you know?" he asks, pulling a red shirt over his head.

I shrug then put my own shirt on and flip my hair out of the collar. "I'm not sure. He said he might call me this morning but all I got was another text from stalker guy."

He frowns. "Did you tell the detective about those?"

I nod. "He's looking into it."

He presses his lips together as if he wants to say something, but then thinks against it and starts wandering around the room, picking up his stuff and packing his bag. I start packing, too, not bothering to fold my clothes. It's actually a habit I picked up from when I was younger. After packing for the fifth time to change homes, I gave up and just stuffed everything in it, not bothering to unpack when I got to my new home.

"You think it's about my mom?" Luke asks so suddenly it throws me off guard and takes me a moment to respond. "What the detective can't tell you yet? Do you think it has something to do with my mom?"

I zip my bag shut and pick it up. "I wonder... maybe."

"I hope it is," he says, anger lacing his tone. I know that he means it—that he wants her locked up just as much as I do. He swings the bag over his shoulder, his muscles jerking a little as if they're sore. Then he walks up to me and gives me a soft kiss on the cheek. "You ready?" he asks, tucking a strand of hair behind my ear and looking me steadily in the eye. It seems like he's asking me much more than if I'm ready to leave his uncle's house. Like if I'm ready to go back to Laramie. To live with him.

I nod, not sure which question I'm answering, but I guess I'll find out when we get there.

***

Luke's uncle seems really upset when we walk downstairs to leave, arguing with Luke over wanting to call his father and borrow some money. Luke says nothing about the fact that he already, I guess deciding to let Cole clean up his own mess. Irate, Cole stumbles over to the coffee table in the living room and chugs about a half a bottle of Vodka. "To ease the pain of the beating," he says when he notices us watching him. Then he flops down on the sofa and moments later he passes out.

Ryler seems like he wants to go with us, just to get out of the house, lingering in the foyer as Luke drops his bag onto the floor to give him one of those awkward one-armed hugs guys do.

"You can come hangout with us whenever," Luke tells him, pulling back and picking up his bag, his eyes drifting to the living room where Cole's on his back, his arm dangling over the side of the sofa. "Even if it's just for a break."

Ryler smiles but it doesn't quite reach his eyes as he lifts his hands, *What the hell would I do in Wyoming?*

Luke looks to me for translation and when I pass a long the message, he says, "The university's pretty cool there."

He raises his pierced eyebrow, amused. *Me go to school? That's a funny idea. I barely made it through high school.*

"Hey, I was the same way. In fact, I almost dropped out," I tell him, feeling strange that I'm talking about my past so lightly. "And I actually like college."

Really? He mouths and I nod. He pauses, looking back at his dad who was never there for him growing up, beaten up and passed out drunk on the sofa and then mouths to me, *Maybe one day.*

I nod then he gives Luke and me his phone number and we finish saying good-bye. With that, Luke and I hit the road. It's early, the sky glowing orange from the sunrise, which means we should get there before sunset. We're a few days earlier than we planned, which means we'll be missing less classes—I think Luke and I can both appreciate that fact. We spend half the drive listening to his music and he playfully tells me he's going to make us a fuck tape of our own when we get home. He keeps saying *we* and I know I should be grateful that I have a place to live with people who care about me, but it's scaring me at the same time. God, if only I could just have one more moment with my parents so they could tell me that this is all okay. That I'm doing the right thing.

As I'm in the middle of this thought, my phone starts to vibrate from inside my pocket. I quickly turn down the music and take out my phone, letting out a breath of relief when I see the screen. "It's the detective," I tell Luke and he nods, looking as nervous as me.

"Please say you can tell me now," I say as I put the phone up to my ear.

"I can, but it's both good and bad news," he tells me, sounding a bit disheartened. "The good news is I finally got that warrant to search Mira Price's home. And we found something that could be potentially useful but we'll still need to run some DNA tests right now to confirm." He gives a long pause. "And then there's the bad news. Two bad newes actually."

"That's not even a word." I make a joke to attempt to hide my true feelings. That I'm excited and terrified at the same time. They might have evidence. My parents might finally have justice.

Luke gives me a concerned sideways glance as he steers the truck down the freeway. "Is everything okay?" he whispers.

I shrug and whisper back, "I'll let you know in a minute."

"Well, I'm declaring it a word for this conversation," he says and then sighs, losing all humor. "The first bad news is that Mira is MIA and from talking to the neighbors and landlord, she's been gone for a while."

I glance over at Luke, wondering if he might know where she is. "So what does that mean exactly?"

"It means that even if we can make the arrest, we have to find her first."

I want to hit something. Scream until my lungs burst. *This isn't fair! This isn't fair. God dammit!* "And what's the second thing?" My voice shakes as my pulse hammers.

It takes him a second or two to answer and when he does, he sounds reluctant. "We found out who's been sending those texts to you... We tracked the calls to Preston Parkington, the guy you've been living with."

"What?" I exclaim, ready to bombard him with questions and Luke's head whips in my direction. "But that's not even possible... how could he... I don't get it..." What the hell? Is this my punishment? For messing up?

"It gets worse," Detective Stephner says. "Due to the threatening material in the text, we were in the right to go to his house and question him, but the trailer had been vacated when we got there."

"But he was just living there a few days ago... I was there... I saw him." My heart is thrashing in my chest, my pulse soaring a million miles a minute and I hate the adrenaline rush inside me right now, so much. "He has to be doing this to get back at me, because I left."

"That's what I thought too, but then I started doing some research on him, a background check and what not and found out a few things that have brought up a big concern."

"Like what?"

"Like he has a record. The fact that he changed his name about fourteen years ago and he's been lying to you about his age. He's thirty-five and used to go by Danny Huntersonly."

"But why would he change his name?" I shake my head, trying to ignore Luke's worried look boring into the side of my head. "And why would child services ever let him take me in?"

"Well, technically the papers state that his girlfriend took you in. A Kelley Arlingford was registered with the state to foster parent."

"Kelley was his wife." I grip the door handle for support because I'm veering toward hyperventilation and feel like I'm going to pass out. "When she introduced him to me, she said Preston was her husband and then they got divorced and Preston was talking about how a while ago she was getting remarried." As soon as I say it though, I know there's a huge flaw. Because most of my information comes from Preston, so therefore there's a chance almost everything could be a lie.

"Well, she was lying to you then, and the state apparently," he says. "In your records, Kelley lived alone and the state didn't even know about Preston, at least from the reports. It's kind of a flaw in the system I guess, not making sure there was no one living with her. But when children get to be that old... and there's so many of them... sometimes they slip through the cracks." He's telling me stuff I already know, since I lived in those cracks for years.

"Did Kelley know about Preston? I mean, did she know about his name change and past?"

"I don't know, but we're going to try to find out." Another pause. "There's more."

"Oh God." My head falls forward and Luke's hand slides across the seat, his fingers lace through mine, and I hold onto him for dear life. "I don't think I can take anymore."

"You need to hear this," the detective says. "You need to understand the severity."

"Fine." I clutch onto Luke's hand so tightly I'm sure it hurts. "Go head."

"Did you know Preston had a secret room under his house in the crawl space."

"Yeah… well, no…" Shit. What do I say? That I knew he kept drugs there. "Well, he kept it locked but I knew that it existed. Wait there was an actual room?"

"Yeah… I figured you didn't know about it, considering what was in there."

"Which was what?"

Another pause. I'm beginning to hate the silence. "A room with pictures and articles of you all over the wall… even some of your parents."

"I don't understand… why would he have that?" I mean, I know he wanted me and everything but that seems like the move of a stalker… "Why is he doing this? It doesn't make any sense? I mean, he was always a little weird and controlling, but why all of a sudden would he resort to threatening texts and a crazy room full of pictures?"

He sighs again and I prepare myself for another blow to the gut. "Violet, I'm not sure how much you know about your parents, but back in the beginning of the case there were few suggestions that no one ever really mentioned to you, simply because you were too young and honestly we didn't want it getting out to the public. Keeping certain details a secret can better help us convict the right person. However, now I think you might need to know, but I want you to prepare yourself for it."

"Okay, I'm prepared." Biggest lie I ever told and I wouldn't have had the guts to say it if I would have known what he was going to say next.

"During the first investigation of your parents, the lead detective on the case found some details about your parents—well, your mother anyway—that connected them to a few local drug dealers. It was a past thing, I think that ended a few years after you were born when your mother married your father."

"No, my mother married my dad before I was born," I say, but really I have no idea—I barely no anything about them, having lost them at such a young age.

266

"No, she married him when you were about three-years-old," he says. "After she got her act together and got out of rehab, but her past was still chasing her and she owed the wrong people some money. The police were never quite able to track down the people in question and honestly all evidence pointed to a random burglary, but after digging into Preston's previous records, I discovered he was living in the Cheyenne area at the time and dealing drugs… and some of the pictures he had of you… you were younger."

"No… you're fucking lying." I shake my head over and over until I get dizzy. "You're lying, you're lying, you're lying. I didn't live with my parent's killer. That would never happen." *Unless it was done on purpose? Oh my God, was it somehow done on purpose by Preston?*

"I'm not saying he's their killer in any way shape or form," he says in a gentle voice. "It's more than likely that he might have developed an obsession with you since most of what we found points toward stalker behavior, which happens sometimes with public cases like these, but I want you to have the details now, just in case."

Just in case what?

Just in case what?

Just in case what?

267

The words echo inside my head over and over again until suddenly I'm seeing Preston's face in the memory, the one where I'm in the basement and he's yelling at Mira Price while she sings and sings and sings. So clearly. But is it just because it was suggested or did I finally put the pieces together.

"No! My mom never did drugs... they were good people..." And to me, the six-year-old with beautiful dreams, they were. They were perfect. And I want to remember them that way. I want to erase everything he said, forget I ever heard it, but I can't.

"I'm not saying they were bad," he tells me. "People that do drugs aren't necessarily bad people. They just made some bad choices and your mother cleaned up her act. She just struggled to erase her past."

Like mother like daughter.

"Violet, I need to ask you some more questions about Preston and what's been going on while you've been living there with him." A pause. "It's important in order for us to track him down."

I can't breathe. Can't think. Can't see. Everything is spinning, round and round and round. All mixed up. All wrong. I can feel the truck pulling over as I gasp for air. As soon as it stops, I drop the phone onto seat, open the door, and fall out of the truck onto my knees. Gravel splits open my knees and the palms of my hand as I dry heave, gasping for air that my lungs won't give me.

Adrenaline overload. One I didn't cause. But one that feels like it's going to kill me. And honestly, I wish it would.

Chapter 16

Luke

She's scaring the shit out of me. She won't talk. Will barely move. I have to lift her back into the truck just to get her off the side of the road. Once I get her inside and get the door shut, I climb in the driver's side then pick up her phone off the seat, which has been ringing since she dropped it.

"Hello?" I answer, my arm moving around Violet as she lowers herself down onto the seat and places her head on my lap. She clutches onto my jeans, still not moving, barely blinking as she stares ahead into nothingness as if she's completely and utterly lost.

"Who is this?" someone asks on the other end of the line.

"Luke… Price."

"Oh…" He sounds uneasy. "This is Detective Stephner. Is Violet there with you?"

"She is but she can't talk right now," I tell him, smoothing my hand over her head, which seems to be helping, her breathing settling, but her eyes are still so hollow. "What exactly did you say to her?"

"I'm not at liberty to tell you that." He pauses. "Are you guys back in Laramie yet?"

I glance at the road in front of us. "No, we're headed back now and are about halfway there... why?"

"Well, I would suggest turning around and taking Violet with you to stay somewhere else just for a few days," he says. "Just until we can get some answers about someone."

I continue to run my fingers up and down Violets cheek and she nuzzles into my touch. "Does this have anything to do with my mother?" I ask quietly.

"You need to talk to Violet. That's all I'm going to say," he replies in a formal tone. "Have her call me as soon as she calms down."

"Okay," I tell him then we hang up. Then I put the phone on the dashboard and stare down at her; her head on my lap, her eyes so full of fear. "Baby do you want to talk about it?" I ask, fighting to keep my voice even. I don't want to push her, but I'm desperate to know if this has to do with my mother.

She shakes her head and closes her eyes as my fingers comb through her hair. "No, not yet."

271

My hand pauses in her hair. "The detective... he said maybe it'd be better if you stayed away from Laramie for a bit."

"Okay, you can leave me on the side of the road." She's not joking either. In fact, she sounds hopeful that I'll do it.

I'm not sure how long I stay parked on the side of the freeway, trying to figure out what to do—where to take her. Back to Vegas? I don't want to do that, don't want to go back to that kind of environment. There's only one other choice, one I have to swallow back what little pride's left, before I take out the phone and dial my dad's number.

He answers after two rings and I sputter it out before I back out. "Hey, I need another favor."

Epilogue

1 day later...

Luke

My dad lives in the section in San Diego where there are towering, slender townhomes and the streets are sloped and lined with trees. The air smells like the ocean and by the time we arrive there, it's nearing the next night, the sun setting, the sky painted orange and pink.

Violet barely spoke the entire drive and only moved when she got out to go to the bathroom when we stopped at a gas station. I took the opportunity to call Kayden and get coaches number so I could talk to him about missing the first week of practice.

"You know he's weird about that shit," Kayden had said, reminding me just how much I might be screwing up my perfect schedule that I'd worked so hard to maintain.

"I know," I'd replied. "But it is what it is... I can't make it there."

"Can I ask why?"

I'd exhaled loudly, unsure exactly what to tell him. "Remember when you beat the shit out of Caleb and you told me something along the lines of you were doing it because someone hurt Callie? And you did it without a second thought, even if it meant your own life was going to get screwed up?"

"Yeah…" He was confused and a little uncomfortable, mainly because we don't talk about this kind of stuff.

"Well, I'm not beating anyone up or anything, but someone needs me right now and I really don't give a shit about football or school at the moment," I'd told him. "Only her."

He'd paused. "Is it Violet?"

"Yeah."

Another pause and then he'd said, "Tell coach it's a family emergency. I did that once and even though he was pissed, he let me off the hook."

"Thanks man," I'd said then quickly had to hang up because Violet had returned from the bathroom and I didn't want her to hear what I was doing, worried she'd try to convince me not to do it.

"I bought some skittles," she'd told me as she return to the truck and that was the last thing she said for the last five hours, eventually falling asleep and not even waking up when we arrived at my dad's house—I had to carry her inside.

"I'm worried about her," I tell my dad as I go back into the kitchen after I've taken Violet to the guest bedroom and laid her in the bed. I don't want to leave her alone too long, worried that she'll do something reckless, like she tried to do back at my uncle's during the window incident.

I'm standing in the kitchen with my dad, tired, in desperate need of some sleep and food. I called Seth on the drive here and asked him if my dad could wire some money to his account and then if he could withdraw it and leave it in Geraldson's mailbox per an agreement I made with Geraldson a few minutes before I called Seth.

"Yeah, sure. Whatever will help," he'd replied and then being him he had of course pressed for more details, which I promised I'd tell him later if he did the favor.

It felt sort of strange that I asked Seth for help. A year or so ago I would have asked Kayden to do it, but I guess things change. Seth knows some of the shit that goes on in my life too—not all but some.

"How long has she been like that?" my dad asks, sitting down on one of the barstools with a mug of coffee in his hand. It's so strange seeing him in person again, since it's been about a year from the last time I saw him and the first time I've seen him since I gave him some insight about what my mother did to Amy and me after he left. He looks different. A little more aged, thinning brown hair, more wrinkles, thicker in the waist, but healthier—a stranger that I know and feel uncomfortable around. Thankfully it's late enough that Trevor is in bed. I haven't had any time to prepare myself to meet my dad, let alone his husband.

"Since she talked to the detective on the phone," I say, sinking down on a barstool next to his, my eyelids so heavy I can barely keep them open. I drove straight here, barely making stops to put gas in the truck and I'm ready to crash, sleep off the last day.

"Did it… Was it…" He struggles, nervously glancing around at the kitchen area, which is decorated with art, probably Trevor's. "Was it about Mira?"

"I don't know." I shrug. "She won't talk about it, whatever it is. But the detective I talked to briefly said it might be best if I took her somewhere away from Laramie for a while." I lower my head onto the countertop, the coldness of the surface feeling good against my warm skin. "Jesus, I have no idea what to do. She's scaring me…"

My father puts his hand on my back and I jump, but don't shove it off. "Go get some rest and then I'll help you talk to her in the morning. I'll help you, Luke… I'm here for you…"

There are a million things I want to say at that moment, some rude and some nice, but all I say is, "Thanks," Bbecause I'm tired.

Then I get off the stool and go up to the guest room, ready to collapse in the bed. But instead I find Violet standing by the window, staring out at the street with her arms folded across her chest. I let out a nervous breath and cross the room to her, hesitating before I wrap my arms around her.

She doesn't fight me, doing the opposite and leaning against me, as if I'm the only thing that's holding her up. "They found evidence that might help the arrest with your mom," she says quietly. "But they have to find her first."

"Wait a minute? Find her?" I slant to the side to look her in the eyes. "She's not at the house?"

She shakes her head, refusing to make eye contact with me. "And the landlord and neighbors said she hasn't been there for a while."

My arms tighten around her, worried that she's suddenly going to push away and run, like she did a couple of months ago. "We'll find her," I promise. "No matter what it takes." I kiss the back of her head and she nuzzles into me. "I'll make sure of it."

"There's more." Her voice sounds so hollow, the moonlight reflecting the pain in her eyes, so overwhelming, almost as if the pain possesses her. It's a look that'll haunt me forever. "It's about Preston and my parents... well, my mother anyway."

"Okay." I have no idea where this is going, but I prepare myself for something extremely bad, because of how she reacted in the car and the look on her face right now.

"Apparently that's not even Preston's real name... and he had all these pictures of me and my family in this little room under the house that I'd always thought he kept drugs in.... and he might have been somehow connected to my mother's drug dealer back when she was doing drugs because he lived in the same area... something I didn't know until now..."

A tear slips from her eye and she doesn't bother wiping it away. "Which not only means that my mother wasn't who I've been thinking she was my entire life, but that Preston might have something to do with their deaths... the detective said it's more than likely that it's coincidental and that he's more of a stalker than a murderer.... But fuck... what if he is... what if he had something to do with it?" Another tear and then another. "All that time I spent with him... those things I did... God, I think I'm going to be sick." That's when she starts to cry, tears pouring out of her eyes as her legs give out.

Tears sting at my own eyes. Jesus, life is so unfair. So cruel. To put one person through this much. Holding her weight for her, I scoop her up in my arms and carry her to the bed. I can't even think of anything to say because there are no words that exist for moments like these. Honestly, I can't even believe it's possible. How can one girl's world be so shattered? So broken. So painful. I want to take all of it away for her—I would in a heartbeat if I could. But instead I have to lie here with her in my arms and listen to her break apart, just like I did a couple of months ago when we found out about my mother. Eventually, my own eyes start to water.

"How can they be sure?" I ask, fighting to keep steadiness in my voice. "The police, I mean. They're going to find out if he had anything to do with it or not, right?"

"Yeah." She buries her face in my chest. "What if he is… what if I let him touch me the way that he did and that whole time he took their lives..." Her hands find the bottom of my shirt and she grips it tightly. "I can't deal with this anymore…" She sucks in a breath, then another. "Pain. I'm so sick of having no one… of having every relationship ruined."

My arms tighten around her and I hold her with every part of me. "No matter what happens, I'm going to be here for you."

She presses her face closer to my chest, balling herself up against me. "Promise me you'll never leave me." It's hard to hear her through the crying, but the soft utter of the words are enough that a few tears escape my eyes. I want to wipe them away so she can't see me falling apart, but I don't want to let her go either.

"I promise." I mean it more than I've meant anything in my entire life. "No matter what happens, I'll always be here for you."

I want to tell her right there that I love her, but know it's in no way the right time. So instead I try to show her, holding onto her and letting her cry, vowing to myself to try to find a way to take some of her pain away, no matter what it takes.

Jessica Sorensen is a *New York Times* and *USA Today* best-selling author that lives in the snowy mountains of Wyoming. When she's not writing, she spends her time reading and hanging out with her family.

Other books by Jessica Sorensen:

Shattered Promises (Shattered Promises, #1)

Fractured Souls (Shattered Promises, #2)

The Coincidence of Callie and Kayden (The Coincidence, #1)

The Destiny of Violet and Luke (The Coincidence, #3)

Breaking Nova (Nova, #1)

The Secret of Ella and Micha (The Secret, #1)

The Fallen Star (Fallen Star Series, Book 1)

The Underworld (Fallen Star Series, Book 2)

The Vision (Fallen Star Series, Book 3)

The Promise (Fallen Star Series, Book 4)

Darkness Falls (Darkness Falls Series, Book 1)

Darkness Breaks (Darkness Falls Series, Book 2)

Ember (Death Collectors, Book 1)

Connect with me online:

jessicasorensen.com

http://www.facebook.com/pages/Jessica-Sorensen/165335743524509

https://twitter.com/#!/jessFallenStar

Made in the USA
Charleston, SC
09 August 2014